THE QUELLING EYE

THE QUELLING EYE
John Gordon

THE BODLEY HEAD
LONDON

British Library Cataloguing
in Publication Data
Gordon, John, 1925—
The quelling eye.
I. Title
823'.914[J] PZ7
ISBN 0-370-31011-x

Copyright © John Gordon 1986
Printed in Finland for
The Bodley Head Ltd
32 Bedford Square, London wc1b 3el
by Werner Söderström Oy
First published 1986

For Dennis and for the Gordon clan—
Norman and Joyce, David and Audrey,
Elizabeth and John, Frank and Maggie.

CONTENTS

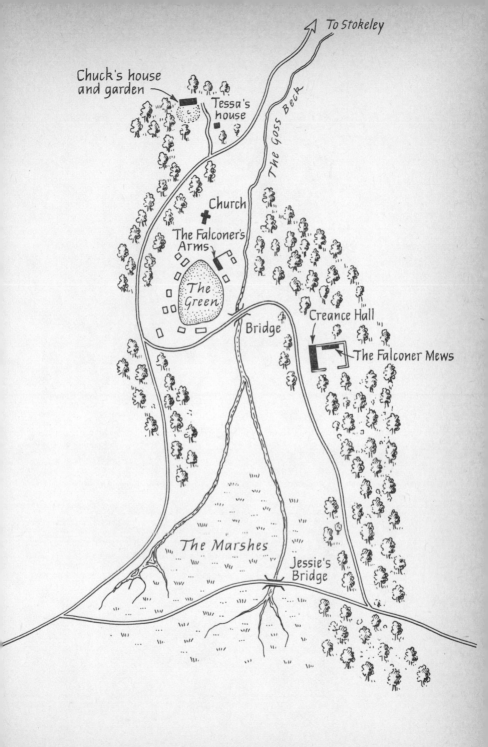

1
The Pond

That day, in just a couple of minutes, a lot of things happened to me. They must have been brewing up, but it didn't feel like it. It was true that the valley was full of sunshine that seemed to be so thick you could almost touch it and taste it, but in summertime this place is often like that. The sun puts great invisible doors of heat across the roadways leading up to where we live, and even though cars and vans do move through the barrier without seeing it, they are in a different place and nothing is quite the same as outside. You might never notice it, but it's true.

It is also true that my father once stole an aeroplane and that my name isn't really Hoskins as people think, but those are quite insignificant things when you put them alongside what happened to us in that honey-coloured heat in June.

Us. That's me, Chuck Hoskins, and the other one, the more important one, who is Tessa Barton. She . . . well, I would like to describe her, but I'll leave that for a little while to tell you something else, because it's important you should know I live in an old house that's high on the hillside near the head of the valley, and Tessa lives in a smaller house down the hill from us. When you're on our lawn, which juts out from the hillside and then drops away sharply, you can see the chimneys of her house above the treetops below, but that's all. There's a lane that comes up from the road and curves round to where she lives before it climbs up to us, and then it stops.

So you might say we're isolated up here, but it doesn't feel like it because we've got this terrific view, which is why my father always said he bought the house. You can see the whole valley and the village and the stream down below like a model.

'Charles!'

That was my mother, Trudy Hoskins, downstairs. I didn't answer, partly because I don't like being called Charles and partly because I was watching a man walking in the sky.

'Charles, I know you're up there. Come down this minute!'

The strange thing about the man was that I didn't know him. I had often seen people walking in the sky because that's what they seem to do when they're right at the edge of the lawn and you get them at the correct angle, which I always do if I can. But I hadn't seen this man before.

'If I have to come up those stairs you'll know about it, my lad!'

And the man was not just walking in the sky, he was trying to fly. He was jumping up and flapping his arms—on *our* lawn, just as if we didn't exist.

'I'm coming up!'

This time her tone was red alert, so I dived out of my room to the top of the stairs and shouted down, 'There's a bird man in the garden!'

Generally, when I say something stupid like that I get the better of her because she starts to laugh, but this time she only said, 'A what?'

'A bird man,' I told her. 'Flapping his arms and jumping about as though he owns the place.' That made her look alarmed, but it should have been me, really, because of what was about to happen.

The next thing I did was pretty brave—braver than I meant it to be, as a matter of fact, but that's my dad's fault. He was always *expecting* me to be brave, even when I didn't feel like it.

What I did was I charged straight outside. The bird man must have heard me coming because he had stopped flapping his arms and was gazing into a little pool in the middle of the lawn as though he was really interested in it, which was ridiculous because it wasn't a proper pond at all, just a little hollow with a few flat stones around it, and it had filled up with rain after a thunderstorm in the middle of the night.

He wasn't a very big man; in fact he was quite small. And he was very neat. I mean he had this light grey suit all buttoned up so it fitted him very close, and he had a lot of white hair that was smoothed back, and quite a long face with wrinkles, but *neat* wrinkles like the outside of a walnut shell. He had a big head, and very big hands.

He didn't look up, even though he must have heard me coming, and I was just about to clear my throat or something stupid like that when he did something really clumsy. He stooped to look into the pool and a shiny object fell from his pocket or his sleeve, I couldn't tell which, and splashed into the water.

I will admit I was feeling just a bit nervous so I didn't shout at him. What I did was very polite. I darted forward and shoved my hand into the pool and picked up the thing, whatever it was, and was handing it to him just as Trudy came up behind me and started being very polite as well.

'Can I help you?' she said.

I remember seeing him smile at her because all his little wrinkles suddenly grew deeper like a photograph coming into focus, and then I looked down at what it was I'd picked up. It was a chain, but quite a bit bigger than the sort of chain some men wear round their wrists, which is why it might have slipped off, and it had square links – or mostly square. I was screwing up my eyes to see it properly when the sun flashed on the surface of the little pond and dazzled me. It was then that everything changed.

Chuck Hoskins shielded his eyes and turned his head but the dazzle made it impossible for him to see his mother. He heard her say something, and then the buzz of the man's voice in reply, but he could not make out the words. They seemed to be in the air above him, and the brightness of the water had affected his eyes so that the sky was streaked and barred. He seemed to be in a great cage, with the voices outside.

He looked down, trying to clear his head. It was a relief to see that he was still standing and that his feet were on the flat stone, because he had begun to think he had fainted and was lying on the ground. But green streaks and shadows still surrounded him, rising into the sky like huge columns.

He screwed his eyes tight and blinked to rid himself of the dazzle. It did not go. And the green columns remained. They were on every side, towering above him like the flat-bladed leaves of great plants.

He bent his head again. At least he still stood on the stone, but even that was different. It was no longer smooth. It was rough and pitted with holes that were large enough to twist his ankle. And there was something else about it that troubled him. He turned his head cautiously. The stone was no longer something on which he could look down and see all its edges at once; now it stretched away on every side as large as a market square. But a market square fringed with tall plants.

Even before he saw the beetle thrust its head between the glossy stems of the plants he knew what had happened. He was no longer his true size. He had shrunk to the size of his own fingernail, and the beetle that was thrusting its shining body through the grass at the edge of the stone had jaws big enough to crush him.

2

Paradise for Sale

It's not true to say that I knew right from the start that I'd gone small. At first I thought I had collapsed in a heap for some reason and was seeing the beetle so huge because my eye was right next to the ground. It was when I jerked my head back to get away from it that I realized what had happened, because then I saw I was standing upright and this great creature was as big as me. I still thought it was some sort of dream, but I was taking no chances. I ran.

The beetle's black shell was like a boat turned upside down and it rocked as all those legs came jerking forward. It was coming very fast.

There was only one side of the stone that had no barrier of grass so I ran for that even though there seemed to be a big blue cliff there that rose up out of sight. I wasn't going to try to climb it—I was thinking like mad as I was running and I knew I couldn't go straight up a wall as fast as a beetle—but I saw something lying on the ground that I thought I could use as a weapon. It was a metal tube about as long as myself. I reckoned that if I could lift it I could fight.

I had to be quick because I could hear the beetle's claws scratching not far behind and I was stumbling a bit because the stone was rough, but there were yellow patches that were springy and I realized that this was some sort of fungus so I kept to that as much as I could. I was doing that sort of thing all the time, recognizing things, and I even saw what the iron bar was, and I panicked. I'd never be able to lift it, not completely, because it was attached to something.

What I was looking at was the metal tag on the end of a shoelace. I saw the lace, and I even saw the shoe behind it, but I didn't recognize the cliffs. Which I should have done, because . . .

I was too busy to think about it. All I knew was that I got to the tag, got a grip on it and heaved it up. Just in time.

I suppose the beetle's back was about the height of my waist, but when its head came up it was as tall as me. There's a lot of moving parts in a beetle's mouth and they're working all the time like machinery, but the big black pincers were worst. They were held wide and they were pointed and they were coming together. On me.

It took both arms to hold that metal bar, but in that second I had extra strength. The gleaming head was like a helmet with horns and I struck down at it with all my force. The bar jarred as it hit and then the pincers swiped together. They clashed on my club, clamped on to it, and the next thing I knew it was wrenched away from me and I was sent flying.

I got to my feet and just scrambled anywhere, so long as it was in the other direction, and I found myself clinging to the shoelace. It was one of those woven ones, but so huge I could get my fingers between the strands, even my feet, and I began to climb.

I looked back just once, and there was the beetle below, still wrestling with the tag, and then I concentrated on getting to the top of the shoe.

Whether I did get there or not I don't know because I don't remember it. I must have fainted again or something. Fainted upwards, because the next instant I was full size and there was the bird man in front of me, saying something.

'Ah, so there you are, young man. I thought you'd left us for a moment.'

'I think I did,' I said.

And then Trudy butted in. 'What's got into you, Charles, daydreaming like that?'

'I must have been,' I said. But it all felt so real I thought I must have had a standing-up faint, a bit of a dizzy patch. 'But I'm all right, now,' I told them. 'Ready for anything.'

I amused the bird man for some reason. He had wrinkled up his face and his grin was so wide I could see his side teeth. 'This is a boy,' he said, 'who would fight lions to guard his mother. A guardian of a boy if ever I saw one.'

I didn't think much of that coming from him. I'm thirteen, but he wasn't very much bigger. I could certainly guard Trudy against him, and I felt like saying so, especially when he got really personal.

'Such a boy would know if his mother was worried about anything, I expect?' His voice was unusual. It had a buzz in it as though whenever he spoke it set invisible piano strings humming. He looked at me with his eyebrows raised, and when I didn't say anything, he just kept on. 'Such a boy would know if his mother was worried, say, about money?'

'I expect he would,' I said, 'if she ever told him.'

'Hum-hum.' It was just as though he was strumming on his invisible strings, and he was still smiling. 'A boy who gives nothing away. A locked-box of a boy. Would he, I wonder, like another secret to add to his store? Something valuable; worth a bit?'

I shrugged my shoulders. I didn't know what to make of him and I was feeling peculiar about the beetle, and me fainting on my feet. But his voice kept buzzing on.

'I can let this boy know that there is a way that all worry can be lifted from his mother's shoulders. I can let him know that he and his mother can have enough money, enough *ten*-pound notes, enough *twenty*-pound notes, enough *fifty*-pound notes to banish all care for ever. What does he think about that?'

I didn't think much of this way of talking about me as though I was two people, but I wasn't given a chance to tell him because Trudy came in fast to stop me. She's always saying I say too much. 'He wants to buy our house,

Charles. He thinks it's for sale. Isn't that ridiculous?'

My mother isn't all that old, I suppose, and sometimes she looks very young. As she did now. She stared at me, frowning a bit, just as though she was my age and was trying to say something with her eyes instead of out loud. I couldn't understand her, but I did know we weren't going to sell the house.

'Very ridiculous,' I said. 'Dad would never want us to move, would he?'

It didn't seem to be exactly what she wanted me to say, but she turned back to the bird man. 'There you are. You heard what my son said, Mr . . . ' She left a row of dots for him to fill in his name, but he put a chuckle there instead. 'So we don't intend to sell.'

'Never,' I said. I hadn't ever thought it was possible. And just to hear her saying something about it, even though it wasn't her idea, made me feel ill. I mean, she likes it so much. She told me once she called it paradise when my dad brought her here.

But the bird man was smiling and pulling a paper out of his pocket. 'Come now, Mrs Hoskins, I have all the details. And if you don't intend to sell, why is there a sign down there in the lane?'

He pointed, and I saw it. It was a white board on a white post, and I even thought I could see 'For Sale' painted on it, and it made me mad. I just took off. I went straight over the edge of the lawn and down the bank, slithering and sliding through the bushes until I jumped down into the lane and then I began to pull at the post, heaving it out of the ground.

It was lying flat and I was stamping on it when Tessa found me.

3
'I Know Something'

I didn't tell Tessa Barton that she was prettier than anybody I'd ever seen, but I thought it.

She said, 'You look stupid.'

I kept stamping on the sign. 'I might be a vandal,' I said—crash, crash—'but I ain't stupid.' My foot went right through the board into the nettles. 'And anyway my leg's all stung.'

That made her laugh, and it made her prettier as well. 'Poor little baby,' she said. 'Shall we find him a dock leaf to make it better?'

I rolled up my jeans and we crouched down together in the lane as she helped me hold the cool leaves against my legs. We were close together and I could see that her eyelashes, which were fair, were darker towards the roots, and her eyebrows were the same because the sun had done what it does to corn and made her hair silvery. I told her so, but all she did was shrug, although I noticed that for a while she didn't look at me. She's got long hair and she had pushed it to one side so that it lay along her cheek and broke like a wave over her shoulders, and I wanted to tell her that, but I didn't.

'What did you want to smash up that sign for?' she said.

That seemed too obvious for me, so I said, 'Well wouldn't you, if somebody suddenly turned up and expected to buy your house when it isn't for sale?'

'Ain't it?'

'No!'

'I thought it was when I saw that sign this morning.'

'Well we didn't put it up there. It's a mistake.'

'Oh,' she said, and I could see she didn't believe me and I wanted to be angry with her, but I couldn't. My mother says she looks sulky, but that's only because of the shape of her mouth. As a matter of fact it's perfect.

I said, 'Signs don't mean anything,' but I was beginning to think there was a lot going on I didn't know anything about. I even thought I might be having another standing-up faint. But that was just panic. So I started asking her questions. 'You didn't think Trudy was going to sell our house, did you?'

She didn't answer, so I said. 'Did you?'

She was a bit careful the way she looked at me and then she said, very slowly, 'We was wondering if you could afford it, Chuck, after your father . . . I mean, just you and your mother.'

You know how a very young kid stares at you and you can't tell what's going on in its mind, well she has the same sort of eyes, blue, and you can't tell what's behind the black dot. 'I'm sorry, Chuck. I'm ever so sorry,' she said.

Tessa Barton longed to take her words back. Why, just at this time, did she have to remind him that his father was dead? He and his mother must be short of money. Everybody said so.

She watched him turn his head away from her, and she didn't blame him. She was just about to speak again when he moved suddenly and made her jump. He was pointing up the slope of the lane.

'Here comes the bird man,' he said, 'and I don't want to see him any more.'

'Bird man?' At the far end of the long channel of trees she saw a grey figure with a shock of white hair step out into the lane, but Chuck pulled her towards the bank and put him out of sight.

'He was dancin' about on our grass, tryin' to fly.' Chuck began to climb the bank at the side of the lane, pulling her with him. 'It's true. Come on, I'll show you.'

20

It was a relief to be doing something, and she laughed. 'I always said you was mad, Chuck Hoskins. Where're you takin' me?' They were among the bushes of the hillside, and above them it rose steeply, almost a cliff, to the edge of his lawn. 'I ain't going up there. What if your mother should see me?'

'Trudy's too busy chasing him away. She'll never see us coming up this way.'

'I don't care.' Tessa stopped.

He tried to persuade her but she shook her head and he gave in. He sat on the slope, and she smoothed her dress and sat beside him. After a while he said, 'Anyway I suppose we ought to make sure the bird man's out of the way before we go any further.' The trees and bushes were too thick for them to see or hear anything that happened in the lane and he did not even pretend to try. Something else was on his mind. 'Trudy's all right,' he said.

'I know she is, Chuck. She must be to let you call her Trudy—I can't see my mum lettin' me call her by her first name.'

'Why not?'

'Why not? That's just you again, ain't it, thinking that everybody everywhere's the same. My mum would have a fit.'

'She'd get used to it, and so would you. Why don't you try practising on Trudy—she wouldn't mind.'

'There you go again!' She tugged at the grass with savage little jerks. 'You're blind, Chuck Hoskins. She'd never *allow* me to do that—ever! Haven't you ever seen the way she looks at me?'

'Just the way she looks at everybody else.'

'Oh, does she! You can't ever have seen her if you think like that. She hates you being with me. She can't stand it, because . . .'

He watched her shredding the grass. 'Because what?'

'You know very well!' She glared at him from under her eyebrows, and her face was flushed. 'It's because you live

21

in that nice house up there, and I live in a sort of builder's yard with all my father's old junk everywhere.'

'Well, he is a builder, ain't he?'

'Sort of. I ain't ashamed.' She was silent for a moment, then she spoke softly, not looking towards him. 'Anyway that ain't it.'

There were no clouds, but he felt as though one had just hidden the sun. 'All right,' he said, 'what is it she don't like?'

'Just listen to yourself and you'd know. You've just said what she don't like. She don't like the way I speak.'

'Too bad!'

'But now you do it as well. I've noticed. Ever since you met me . . . All the time you're getting worse. I've heard it, so it's no good you denying it. And another thing,' there was no stopping her now, 'and another thing which I know is true because somebody heard her say it and then told me, is that she thinks I run around with too many people. Boys. That's what she thinks. So you might as well go away and leave me.'

She was pale and clinging with both hands to the grass as though the slope was getting steeper at every instant and was about to fling her off.

'Well, that ain't true,' he said.

'I know it ain't true. There was just that once. Just that once, that's all.'

Chuck's mouth had gone dry, and he had to lick his lips. 'Fletcher?' he said. He knew what she meant. There was something about her and Big Fletch.

'Well, it was just . . .' She refused to plead with him but her voice was filled with anguish. 'There was just that one time when him and his mates was down there,' she tilted her head towards the village, 'and I was there and they was all playing about, and they got rough, and then one of them got hold of me just as your mother came along. She saw me. She must have thought I always did things like that.'

'Like what?' His own misery was as deep as hers.

22

'One of them grabbed me and said something and they all laughed. That's all, Chuck, there weren't nothing else.'

'Who was it?' He heard the hoarseness in his own dry throat. 'What did he say?'

'It was Fletch, and I ain't repeating it because it's all over. Dead and done with.' She began to get to her feet. 'It ain't no good, you and me. I'm going now.'

She moved quickly but he was quicker. He held her wrist and then could only just keep his grip because the slope was steep and they had begun to slither. They were at an awkward angle, staring at each other, and she could see the questions forming in his mind.

'I hate him!' She said it so loudly it was almost a cry. 'I always did hate him! And I don't know why it happened and I don't care whether you believe me or not, just let me go.'

He released her and they sat side by side, not looking at each other. He wanted to tell her that it didn't matter, but the words would not come. It did matter. What he longed to be able to do was to go back with her and stop it happening, wipe it out. The sun shone on them for a long minute before either of them spoke.

'Tessa.'

'Yes?'

He had just wanted to speak her name. He had nothing to say. There was silence again, and then she heard him ask, 'Do you believe in magic?'

'I might do.'

'Well, I know something,' he said.

4

Tessa

When Chuck Hoskins asked me about magic I wasn't surprised. Nothing he says surprises me, but it wasn't just that. I know he's a bit nutty, and for a long time I was just like Josie Jones and used to laugh at him, sort of, but then I got to know about his father and that was so *interesting* I began to change my mind about him, and once I started doing that I found we thought about some things in the same way. A secret way it was—well it still is—and I'd never told anybody.

I mean, round about that time I'd started thinking about the village and everything in a most peculiar way. I kept imagining the whole valley was like a pop-up book, opening up with the village in the fold down the middle, and the houses looked like gingerbread houses, and all the passages led to courtyards with magic doorways that opened up into secret gardens. I felt like that all the time, and even the air seemed to be gold dust, so I knew something strange was going to happen. I just didn't know how strange it was going to be.

The trouble was he was taking me up towards his house and his mother made me nervous. That was another thing that wasn't the same as it had been. She used to like me a lot, and then Chuck started coming to see me every minute of the day, and she changed. It was very sudden. One minute she liked me, and the next she was so cold it was horrible. So I was worried in case she was there when we came up the steep sides of his lawn. But Chuck wasn't. He gives a pretty good imitation of being tough, and I think he is brave, but he don't believe it himself. So he's always unsure, like being halfway through a door and half way not, so you never know about him. He's wild one minute, and then for a whole day he's very quiet. It's the quiet girls that seem to like him best, but he generally seems to go for the loud ones.

His lawn is like a big half-circle jutting out from the hillside, and right in the middle was this little pond made by the rain in the middle of the night, but I didn't bother about it because I was looking up towards the house. There's a huge flowerbed at the back of the lawn and you have to go up some steps right through it and then go across some crazy paving before you come to the house, and then it's all little windows and long low thatch like eyebrows. I was trying to make out if there was anybody up there when he took me around the pond and made me stand with my back to the house and all those windows that were peeping through the flowers.

'Hey!' he said, 'you got to look this way,' because I was turning my head over my shoulder. 'Watch the water.'

'Why ain't you watching it?' I said because I could see he was shielding his eyes.

'Because I want to see what happens.'

'To me?' I said, but then I could hardly see him because with his other hand he made ripples in the water and the sun flashed in my eyes and dazzled me. He did it again. I said, 'What are you doing?'

'Do you feel any different?'

'In what way?' I said. 'How do you want me to be different?' I wanted to help him and I could see he was very disappointed that nothing had happened.

He didn't answer. He was looking down towards my feet at the big stone slab I was standing on, and he was talking to himself. I heard him say, 'Well at least I know what the blue cliffs were.'

Blue cliffs? I didn't have any idea what he was talking about and I told him so.

That made him look up. Sometimes people think he's my

25

brother because his hair is my colour, almost, but his face isn't the same. It's quite a big face and slightly lopsided, and sometimes he's a bit scruffy, which I don't mind. At least he's not normal like everybody else. But I didn't understand blue cliffs.

'My jeans,' he said. 'The legs of my jeans were blue cliffs when I was down there.' He was pointing at my feet again and grinning a bit, but he soon stopped doing that. 'I'm sure it happened, Tessa. I'm sure it did.'

I had no idea what he was talking about and I was getting exasperated, but still he wouldn't tell me what he was hoping to see.

'I've got to see if it happens even if you don't know about it,' he said. 'I don't want you just to imagine it. It's a controlled experiment.'

Controlled experiment! 'What's controlled about magic?' I said. 'You can't control it—it just happens.' I was thinking about the valley and him and me seeing it in a different way to everybody else and I didn't want to spoil it by thinking about it. I thought I knew more about that kind of thing than he did but it was too late to stop him.

He stood up, talking more to himself than to me. 'There was that funny bit of chain,' he said, 'which he dropped in the water, and then I went to pick it up.' He bent over as though he was doing the same thing, but before he touched the water he stood up straight again and began to search in his pockets. 'I haven't got any chain just at the moment,' he mumbled.

Well I didn't suppose he had, but I don't think he noticed I was being sarcastic because he was saying to himself, 'Well perhaps it doesn't have to be a chain. A chain is only rings.'

'Just one damned ring after another,' I said, but I don't think he heard me.

'And I'm sure that when the water flashed I saw it through one of those rings.' He looked at me for a minute. 'Tessa . . .?'

I waited.

'Are you wearing a ring?'

I showed him. There's a little silver ring my granny gave me when I was quite small and I hardly ever take it off.

'Will you give it to me, Tessa?'

Sometimes, when he's a bit shy, he sort of puffs his face up so he looks like a battered baby. You could never be unkind to him. So I gave him the ring, and he dropped it straight in the water. I think I started to laugh, but it was excitement more than anything. What he was doing was serious, even if it was mad.

'Will you pick it out, Tessa? And when you do that, will you look through it? Will you, Tessa?'

He was saying my name over and over, and I knew he wanted the same thing to happen to me as had happened to him—so I did, but I didn't know what it was. So I crouched down.

I could see the ring on the grass under the water, and just for a moment I was afraid of it. I think I was afraid that nothing would happen, that it didn't mean anything, and the pop-up village down below was only cardboard. But suddenly I thought a cardboard village is a kind of magic, not at all what it seems to be, and perhaps my ring was something similar. So I reached into that water and I picked it out.

I had to squint a bit to see it properly because the sun was caught up on the ripples and making flashes so bright I thought I could hear them hiss. Like lightning before the thunder comes.

That's what I thought, and I was still thinking it as I began to fall. It wasn't ordinary falling, but a long slow glide, and I thought I had passed out because I was cold. Then the next second I was lifted up, lying on my back, and all I could see was the sky, and everywhere around me there was glaring light. I was in a blaze of it, dazzled out of my mind.

Then I was tilted again. There was nothing I could do

about it, but as my head came up and my feet went down I realized what was happening. I was in water, floating on my back as though I had been gently laid there, so gently that my face wasn't even wet, and the glaring light that came and went was the sun spilling over huge smooth waves that were pushing me towards what looked like a forest.

I saw the forest and at practically the same time I saw something else, and this was an even bigger surprise, but in a funny way I seemed to expect it. I knew what had happened to me. I had shrunk to something no bigger than the ring I had fished from the water, and I was lying on the surface of the pond—or else I'd been dazzled so much I thought it had happened, because the other thing I saw, high overhead against the sky, was a huge hand and arm, and then further away a great solemn face and long fair hair. I was looking up at myself, my big self, crouching at the edge and looking down into the pond.

Of course, it was all a trick that Chuck had worked somehow, so I took a deep breath and held it because I wanted it to last a bit longer. I couldn't believe I was really looking up at myself and at the same time lying as light as a leaf on the surface of the pond. But it seemed so real it was my turn to try an experiment.

My hand lay on the water but didn't seem to penetrate it. It lay on the water but it wasn't wet because there was a film over the water, a sort of transparent skin that was swimming with colours like the surface of a bubble, and when I pressed it with my hand it trembled but did not break. It seemed so real it was cleverer than anything I had ever seen.

'How did you do it, Chuck?' I said. I couldn't see him but he had to be there. 'Chuck, where are you?'

I dug my fingers into the wobbling surface, and that was a mistake. They went through. There was a gentle plop as the surface just seemed to crack all over and I was swimming, yelling at the top of my voice, then going

28

under. I can swim, but not very well, and when I came up the shore seemed miles away.

Then a wave broke over me and pushed me around and I saw some humps that rose just above the surface of the water. They seemed to be islands, but they were smooth and pinkish and as rounded as cushions. I didn't know what they were. They might have been dangerous but I was so afraid of drowning I didn't care. I swam towards them and reached out.

I must have touched one of those pinkish cushions but I don't remember it. All I remember is that I was so exhausted I seemed to go to sleep for about a blink—and I woke up to hear somebody speaking.

And I wished I was listening to somebody else.

5

A Secret Kept

Tessa has one way of getting the better of me which I don't suppose she knows about but it happens quite a bit. I never did tell her, but when there was a fair in the village last year and they had those old-fashioned swingboats with ropes I tried to scare her by making our boat go high—but all she did was make it go higher. In the end I had to stand up when we were going *vertical* before she seemed to be the least bit worried. And by that time I was so dead scared I was nearly being sick.

She doesn't know she does it, but she never makes any allowances, and it happened again when we were standing beside the pond and my mother came up to us and began to say something. I knew Tessa didn't want my mother to see her, but I did think she would turn round and speak. I didn't know that anything had happened to her when she picked the ring out of the water; all I knew was that she'd gone a bit quiet and was still crouching beside the pond. Her hand holding the ring had flopped back into the water so I reached for it and helped her stand up. She looked a bit dazed, and I thought it was because she was shy, but then she began to speak and it made everything worse.

'I thought I was drowned,' she said. I still didn't understand, but she did look frightened. 'My head went under and I was rolled over and over. Down there.' She pointed to the pond—and then I guessed. She said, 'I thought I was in the sea. It was like an ocean.'

'Was it, dear?' said my mother. You could tell by the way she said *dear* she wasn't taking anything seriously and it made me mad.

I said to her, 'Trudy, are you listening?'

She said, 'There's no need to shout, Charles. I heard every word.' She was looking up towards the house all the time, never at Tessa. 'And Theresa is quite able to speak for herself. She expresses herself very well.'

'Well why ain't you listenin'?'

I said it like that to annoy her, but I wished I hadn't because it dragged Tessa in as well. Tessa said 'ain't' quite a bit, but I only say it some of the time, and it gave my mother the chance to look as though it caused her real pain and make Tessa feel like an outcast or something. She used to be really nice, did Trudy, but just then she wasn't. She spoiled everything.

'You don't believe anything we've been saying,' I said, and when she looked puzzled I told her all about it, in detail. About the bird man, and how Tessa and me had each gone tiny, even though we were still big at the same time. Just as if we'd slipped out of ourselves.

'Really, Charles!' she said, and she was laughing at me. 'It's true!'

I just about shouted it, but all she did was look at us with a kind of faint little smile and I knew what she was thinking—vivid imaginations, the pair of them, and they're both very young—I could see it in her face. At that minute I didn't like her very much at all, and I said, 'Well why don't you try it!'

She could see I meant it, and she went suddenly serious. She was going to put me in my place, and quick.

'Very well,' she said, and she began to come closer. 'What do you want me to do?'

It angered Trudy Hoskins to see her son holding the girl's hand. They had no right, at their age, to behave like that. And now they were inventing ridiculous stories. It had gone too far. 'Well,' she repeated, 'show me what to do.'

Chuck could feel the ring between Tessa's wet fingers. 'Let me have it, Tess,' he said, but she clung to it tighter, and when he looked at her he saw her face was pale and wild.

'Please, Tess. We've got to prove it. It might be the only chance we get.'

She shook her head so violently her hair swirled and at the same time she spoke directly to his mother, abruptly changing the subject.

'I didn't know you were going to sell your house, Mrs Hoskins.'

'Are we, dear?' Trudy let the little smile leave her face. It was no business of the girl what she intended to do about the house. 'I didn't know you knew so much about us.'

'I saw the sign.' Tessa spoke breathlessly, saying too much. 'I saw Chuck pull it down and stamp on it. His foot went right through, so I don't suppose you *are* going to sell it.' She tried to smile. 'Not really.'

Mrs Hoskins turned a hard eye on her son. 'Is that what you've done, Charles? A ridiculous thing like that?'

He shrugged. 'What's wrong with pulling down a stupid sign, Trudy? I know we're not going to leave.'

She pressed her lips together and let the silence grow. 'You,' she said, 'take far too much upon yourself, young man. You have not the slightest idea of what I intend to do.'

'But Trudy—'

'Don't Trudy me—I'm your mother. And in future I would ask you not to behave so childishly, and particularly I do not want you to spread our private affairs around the whole village.'

She turned her back on them and walked so quickly towards the house they had no chance to reply. It wasn't until the door closed firmly behind her that Chuck let out his breath, but even then he said nothing.

'The whole village.' Tessa repeated his mother's words. 'That means me.'

He remained silent. She could see he was wrestling with

his anger, and she said, 'It's my fault everything's gone wrong. I'm sorry, Chuck.'

'Too late to be sorry. She was all right until you told her about the sign.'

'I couldn't help it. I didn't want her to find out about the pond and everything.'

'Why not? Are you trying to make it into one of those stories where kids discover something but they can't make anybody else believe? Is that what you're trying to do, just make me out to be a little kid?'

'No! It happened to me as well as to you. You're not so special!'

'But you don't want *her* to know.' He was still angry. 'Why not? What's wrong with her?'

'Nothing!'

They glared at each other before Tessa, turning away, spoke so quietly he could hardly hear her. 'I think your mum is ever so pretty,' she said. 'Everybody does, as a matter of fact.'

'What's that got to do with anything?'

She swung towards him. 'You're a fool! You don't understand a single thing that goes on inside people.'

'I can understand that you spoiled everything just now. Just when we had a chance to prove it.'

'It's nothing to do with anybody else.'

'You mean it's a secret?' He was scornful. 'Just you and me?'

'Well why not?' She tried to prevent him tearing everything down. 'Don't you want a secret?'

'No, I don't!'

Chuck saw tears in Tessa's eyes and wanted to tell her what he really felt but she was shaking her head to stop him. 'I said your mum was very pretty, and she is. But she don't like me, and I don't think you do, either.'

He put out a hand but she shook it off and ran away from him.

6

Voices Downstairs

There were voices downstairs. Chuck felt hot under his single sheet and threw it off as he raised himself on one elbow to listen. The whole house, crouching like a badger on the hillside, was silent except for the muffled voices that rose and fell like gentle breathing.

The luminous hands of the clock at his bedside showed it was past midnight, so he must have been asleep a long time. His mother had been alone when he went to bed, but no car grinding up the lane had woken him, and he was sure the doorbell had not rung. She must have been expecting the caller, whoever it was.

Curiosity got him out of bed and he was at his bedroom door just as his mother and her visitor came into the hall. It was a man, but Chuck could not see who it was, and they spoke so softly that all he heard before the outer door opened and they went into the porch was the man saying something that sounded like 'same time, same place', and then his mother's reply was no more than a murmur.

He waited but they lingered so long in the porch and their voices were so indistinct that boredom drove him to lie down on his bed. He carefully left his door ajar hoping she would see it when eventually she climbed the stairs and would come in to see him. Then they could be friendly again, and he would be able to find out who it was downstairs with her now. He knew there was no risk he would fall asleep as he waited because there was too much on his mind to allow it, and once he suddenly found himself sitting upright, struck by the thought that at this

34

very moment she was making a deal to sell the house. A moment later, however, he slumped back on his pillow. Selling the house was not the danger. Whoever it was she was talking to below was not the bird man. The voice did not have the buzzing edge to it, and the stranger's hair, which was all he had seen, was dark, not white.

Then Tessa tugged at his mind. All he could think of, again and again, was the way she had disappeared over the edge of the lawn, going down until only her hair, spread out on her shoulders and catching the sun, was visible. Everything had gone with her. The magic had drained away and the pool was only a pool. He had turned his back. It was useless without her. Whatever had made them both believe for a few seconds that they could change and make the whole world different was gone. He felt he was coming out of a dream that, no matter how hard he tried, refused to let him return to a place where marvellous things were everywhere.

He twisted, sinking his head deep into the pillow and, in spite of everything, he was drifting into sleep when his mother climbed the stairs. He heard her, but he did not wake fully until her door clicked and it was too late.

Now he was wide awake. And so was the night. The house was silent but not quite dark, as though its eyes were open, waiting and watching. His bed lay under the dormer window in the sloping ceiling, but all it showed him was the stars above the roof. Even the moon was hidden.

Chuck's bedroom was at the front of the house and by standing on his bed with his shoulders within the little alcove of the window he could look along the length of the valley. There was a haze down there, lying in strands among the treetops and gathering light from the moon, hoarding it in mid-air and letting only the faintest glimmer get through to the sleeping village.

Directly beneath him the terrace and flowerbed jutted out and hid most of the lawn beyond. Even the little pond was out of sight—if it should still be there and had not seeped away into the dull earth like everything else. Chuck had to find out.

He undid the window catch and, balancing himself on the rail at the foot of his bed, pushed the window open and levered himself through until his stomach rested on the ledge. Still only the far edge of the lawn was visible. He wore no pyjama top and the night air chilled his bare skin as he reached down to the thatch and eased himself further out.

He was high over the valley floor. Behind him the top of the hill humped itself against the sky, but he was clear of its slope, on a perch like a night bird, clutching the sharp reeds in his claws and letting the whole scoop of the valley rest in his eyes. He turned his head like an owl. Beneath him the steps went down through the flowerbed to the platform of the lawn where, in spite of the moon, the little pond was no more than a patch of darkness.

He turned his head to inspect the treetops, and as he did so the wisps of mist that clung to the edge of the lawn seemed to move. It must have been caused by the movement of his head, but when he turned to look again the mist was changing shape. A shadow grew within it. And moved. It drifted sideways, and as it did so he saw what it was. A human figure, cloaked so that its legs were hidden, was gliding through the garden.

Half-naked, the moon shining white on his skin, Chuck gazed over the edge of the roof as the silent shape came to rest. He could not tell whether its head looked out over the valley or whether its hidden face was tilted up and was watching him, waiting with the patience of a falconer trying to tempt down a bird from a high branch.

The whole night was still. Everything was fixed and motionless under the moon. And then Chuck's fingers began to slip on the smooth reeds. He clutched tighter, and the brittle stems crackled in the silent night.

At the same moment the figure moved. It dipped suddenly into a crouch, then raised itself with its arms

36

spread wide and its cloak like dark wings. Chuck pressed down with the heels of his hands to check the slide, hooked his knees behind the window ledge and flung himself backwards into the house and safety. His eye caught a gleam as the cloak touched the surface of the pond and the ripples tossed up silver fragments of moonlight, and then he was falling, twisting head over heels into the darkness of his room.

Or so it seemed. The sense of falling left him. He felt no thud of landing, but he was face down, clinging to a cool, hard surface. He must be flat on the floorboards inside his room. He began to press himself up, but as he did so his knees slid backwards across the boards and he sank. He tried again, but this time it was worse. It was as though the whole floor had tilted and he could not get his balance.

He felt dizzy. Perhaps he had hit his head and was concussed. He raised it cautiously without trying to get up. He could not recognize his room, and he was not lying on floorboards. They were not even flat; they were curved like a layer of huge pipes and he was clinging to one of them. He wrapped his legs and arms around it as far as the pipes alongside it would allow and carefully turned his head. His concussion was worse than he thought, for what he saw turned him giddy. He lay on a slope that seemed made of felled trees, and they stretched down beyond his feet away out of sight into darkness.

He lowered his head slowly, letting it rest on the smooth trunk that pressed against his chest. If he was badly injured he must be careful. For a full minute he lay where he was, trying the movements of his legs and arms. All seemed normal, except for his eyes and what they were showing him. He risked raising his head again. The sky was above him, and stars. He breathed the air. It was cool. Outdoor air. His eyes had not fooled him. He was not in the safety of his room. He was outside.

In that instant he knew what had happened. Bit by bit he tested what he saw. The felled trunks were too smooth for

37

trees and gleamed in the moonlight. And they were hollow. He could see the gaping ends of open tubes above him. They were reeds, gigantic reeds, and they made the thatch of a vast house. He was clinging to its roof, half-naked in the dark. And he knew it was not the house that had grown suddenly into a giant's castle, it was himself that had dwindled, shrunk so small that a fingernail could flick him away.

It had happened again. The flash of light from the pond had dazzled him and separated him from himself. Somewhere indoors, within his room, his normal self was lying motionless, aware of nothing, while the tiny seed of himself that could see and move and think had been left out on the roof. It was as though he was able to move about within a dream.

But this was no dream. The edges of things he touched were too hard, and the slippery fall beneath him was too real. He looked up. Above him, hanging out into space, was what seemed to be a polished wall. It was the glass of his window, wide open and reflecting the moon.

He wedged his feet between the reeds and began to crawl. He slipped and had to cling, but found a rougher surface and went up steadily until, under the overlap of his window ledge, he clutched a crack in the woodwork, heaved himself up and stood on the level surface.

He was panting, gazing back down the slope, when a throbbing in the air made him crouch. He was too late. The pulsing rush of the air was on him. A moth as furry as a flying bear rowed itself out of the night towards him, caught him with the edge of a hard and dusty wing and sent him spinning backwards into the empty darkness of his room.

7

Daylight

Daylight streamed in through the window, but Chuck closed his eyes and tried to cling to the long fall through the shadows of the night. He was again his true size. Whatever had happened must, after all, have been a dream. Anything else was absurd. The moth had been a shape from the edge of sleep that had sent him spinning down to the soft landing on his bed. After that he had a confused memory of seeming to climb on to an enormous hand where he found warmth and eventually slept.

'You're all upside down.' It was his mother. 'Feet on the pillow, and head hanging over the end of the bed. You must have had a funny sort of night.'

'It was,' he said. 'Very funny.' Funnier than anything he could tell her. He was face down, speaking to the carpet, and he did not want to move. He was more than ever certain he had dreamt everything. It had all been inside his head, every scrap of it.

'It's a good job it didn't rain in the night,' she said. 'Your window's wide open.'

The window. He felt the air from it on his back and raised himself to sit cross-legged on his bed. 'You opened it,' he said.

'But not like that. It's not even on its catch.' She was laughing, in a good mood. 'What if an owl flew in?'

'Or a moth. There's one just by your head.'

'Where? Where? I can't stand those things!' She was not tall, and when she bobbed her head and flapped her hands around her black curls she was a girl anybody could tease.

'On the ceiling.' It was large and dark and motionless,

39

spread out like a specimen in a museum. It was not going to threaten her.

'And you,' she advanced on him, ready to tussle, 'you sit there like a young Buddha and frighten me out of my wits. I'll skin you alive!'

It was a long time since she had been like this, her cheeks made rounder by mischief and her black eyes dangerous, but this time he did not let himself be chased around the room. He stood up on his bed and backed away. 'There was somebody here last night,' he said. 'Who was it?'

She stopped in front of him. 'What's it to you, nosey?'

'It was a man.'

'Well what if it was? I can have somebody to see me in my own house, can't I?'

'It's my house as well.'

'Saucy young devil!' She was laughing as she came forward, forcing him to crouch under the slope of the ceiling.

'You're blushing,' he said.

She grappled with him in the way they used to tumble together when he was smaller and in the end she got him to his knees by twisting his fingers.

'You fight just like a girl,' he said. 'That hurts.'

'Well I am a girl, and say you're sorry.'

'I'm not sorry. Ouch.'

'Say I can have who I like in this house.'

'You're hurting!'

'Say it.'

'I will if you let me have who I want.'

'What's that supposed to mean?'

'You don't like Tessa Barton, but I do.'

'Who said I don't like her? I never said anything of the sort.'

'You don't have to say anything. It's obvious.'

'I happen to think she's a very pretty girl, if you want to know.'

He felt her grip loosen and he tugged free. 'But you

don't like the way she talks.' He was watching her carefully as she sat on the end of the bed, no longer wanting to fight him. 'You don't like the place she lives, either. She's not posh enough, is she?'

His mother was not looking at him. 'Well she doesn't sound . . .' She stopped speaking, smoothing out a wrinkle in the sheet then putting it back. She took a quick breath and spoke in a rush. 'I was speaking to somebody just the other day and he said she was rough. She acts rough.'

'Who said?'

'It doesn't matter who. It's just that everybody thinks so. It's not her fault, it's the whole family.'

'You never used to think like that. You was friendly, but now you ain't.'

She looked up sharply. 'That's just what I mean. Did you hear yourself, the way you speak? It's got to stop, Chuck.'

'You mean Charles, don't you?'

'Yes, I do. It's your name, your real name.'

He crouched with his head on one knee, and he began to understand. 'That's why you're going to sell this house,' he said. 'So's I don't have anything to do with her.'

'Don't be ridiculous.' She was angry now. 'You need bringing down to earth, my lad. You're full of nonsense.'

'Not as much as you.'

He had gone too far. 'You'd better be quiet,' she said, and when she saw him open his mouth she raised her voice. 'Not another word!'

But he had nothing left to lose. 'Mum,' he said, 'you're not really going to sell our house to that man, are you?' She stayed silent. 'Because he's mad. He came back in the middle of the night and he was dancing on the lawn again.'

'Charles!' It was a warning.

'But I saw him, and he . . .' It was no good going on. He was even guessing that the cloaked figure—if there had been such a thing—was the man with white hair.

41

'And he what?' Now that she saw his doubts, she was pressing him. 'What did he do?'

'Nothing.'

'That's better.' She stood up. 'And I want no more fairy stories from you. I've had enough!' She went out, and left him punching his pillow.

8

Big Fletch

Dreams and magic were all mixed up, and I didn't know what I believed. I nearly killed myself climbing half out of that window again, looking for proof. The drop seemed even worse in daylight, but I could see the pond if I leant out far enough. Only just. Then I searched the window ledge for evidence, and there was a crack in the woodwork that I could have climbed but there was no dust that looked as if it had come from a moth's wing. I got dressed and out of the house without bothering about breakfast. I had Tessa's silver ring. It fell on the grass when she ran away so I was going down to the pond to try with it, but Trudy was in the garden so I went out and down the lane before she saw me.

The sign was still there, lying flat with a hole through it, so I hadn't dreamt all that. And I was certain about the horrible things I said to Tessa, so when I came to the side track that led to her house I wasn't sure what to do. But I had to see her.

You get to her house through a lot of trees and you can walk quietly, so I was hoping I might be able to watch until she came out alone, but it wasn't any good. She's got this little kid brother, Jago, who's worse than a watchdog. He saw me coming and he slammed the big gate right across the path.

'Tess don't like you no more!' He's got no volume control on his voice, so anybody could have heard. 'She don't like you so you can git!'

I couldn't back away now, so I asked him if she was in the house. 'I've got something that belongs to her,' I said.

Big mistake.

'Give it to me, then.' He's too much of a titch to reach over the gate, so he pushed an arm between the bars. 'Give it over. It ain't yourn.'

I said I wasn't going to give it to him because it belonged to Tessa.

'Mum! There's someone stealing somethin' from Tess! He's a robber!'

His round red face was about the ugliest thing I'd ever seen so I bunged a handful of earth at it and left him yelling his head off. What did I care?

And any way you looked at it, it wasn't going to be my day. Not even when I found Tessa. It only got worse.

She was down by the stream, just where it goes under the road. It's not a proper bridge, more of a tunnel, but there's an iron railing along the road and that's where she was, sitting on it right next to Big Fletch.

He's a lot older than her, and so are his mates, and three of them were making the far bank of the stream look untidy. I'd never seen them before but I could've told they were his lot just by the way they were watching a kid making a dam with stones. They had that eager look, just waiting for him to finish so they could knock it down. Then they'd probably go up to the village to kick in the bus shelter or something else useful. And Fletch was making sure he was in charge.

I knew I was walking straight into trouble but there was nothing I could do. I went down and stood near the kid in the stream. It was Paul White and he's a bit younger than I am, so I was right in the middle. He's a pale little kid anyway, but he was paler than ever and I reckon he was quite brave to keep on pretending he was enjoying himself. I hate seeing people bullied, but the most I reckoned I could do was to stand alongside him. Which I did, quite close.

Tessa was up above the culvert, sitting on the rail. I said, 'I've got something of yours,' but she didn't even look at me. 'I could have left it with your brother, but I didn't.'

Still nothing, and Big Fletch said, 'She don't seem to want to talk to you, Hoskins.'

I ignored him, 'Should I keep it, Tessa, or give it to you later?'

'Na,' he said, 'don't bother. Just give it to me.'

I picked up a pebble and threw it into the culvert. I heard it rattle away and wished I could've gone with it.

'Hoskins.'

Fletch was perched up above with his big boots hooked on the rail. His T-shirt had no sleeves so that his muscles showed. I didn't want anything to happen, so I said nothing.

'Hoskins, I'm talking to ya. What is it you got that belongs to Miss Barton here?'

That was wit, calling her Miss Barton, and all his mates laughed. It was like a football match—they all opened their mouths to bray at the same time, and I lost my temper.

'None of your business,' I said.

I heard his big boots hit the ground, and the next thing I knew he was standing beside me. 'Give,' he said. 'Hand it over.'

It was then that Tessa got frightened. She called out, 'It don't matter, Fletch. I don't want it.'

She was coming to my rescue, but it was too late. He has a big face, has Fletcher, but a tiny little mouth and he'd puckered it up so you could hardly see it. And his eyes were just little bristly bunches of eyelashes. He was being pretty mean, and his mates were watching.

'You been pinchin' things, Hoskins, and I always thought you was a good little boy, didn't I?'

I said nothing.

'I always thought you was a good little boy, but now I see you're a bad little boy.'

His tiny mouth smiled at me, and the thing that I'm most ashamed of is that I smiled back. I did. I was so scared I wanted him to like me, and what he said was, 'A bad little boy, Chuck Hoskins, just like your mother. She's a bad girl nowadays, they tell me.'

Tessa was leaning forward. She yelled at him, 'Shut up, Fletch!'

'See,' he said, 'she knows about Mrs Hoskins and I know about Mrs Hoskins. Don't you know about Mrs Hoskins?'

I saw Tessa's face. It was all twisted up.

'What about my mother?' I said.

'Nothin' much.'

He looked as if he was about to turn away but I shifted to keep in front of him. 'What about her?' I said.

'I don't know as I ought to tell you.'

'Please,' I said. I'm ashamed of that, as well.

'Well "please" is different. Didn't you know about her and her feller? Surely you seen him come around with his tongue hangin' out—every day, just about. You can't blame him, because your mum's his bit of crumpet.'

I wasn't pretending to be brave any longer. He just pushed his sneer right up close to me, and I hit it. He must have been surprised because he left his face where it was, and I hit it again.

I didn't get a chance to do it another time because they all came for me then and I was down on the ground being kicked.

9

A Touch of Danger

Tessa walked backwards in front of him so she could command his eyes. She was excited, almost dancing.

'But did you see him get his lovely boots wet? Oh that was lovely when you hit him—I've never been so scared.'

'Nor me.'

'You wasn't scared! You wasn't scared a bit. I seen your eye go glinty, then swack! That ain't being scared.'

'He shouldn't have said . . .' Chuck hesitated. 'He shouldn't have said what he did.'

'There go your eyes again!' She was laughing but gradually becoming serious. 'I'm glad I ain't him. *And* he's got his boots all wet and full of mud.'

She was walking alongside him now, quite soberly, and he wanted to ask her about his mother and what Big Fletch had said, but the words would not come. 'I hate that Fletch,' he said. 'I hate him.'

'And you won't have no more trouble with him, not after what you done.'

'What about his mates?'

'They ain't from here, and they won't come back—not after what that man done to them. Did you see him come charging down at 'em?'

'I was underneath being kicked, don't forget.'

'Well he saw what was happening to you and he stopped his car and he came flyin' down that bank. You should've seen them scatter. Falling over in the mud and everything. I did enjoy it!'

Chuck felt good. 'He left his car door open didn't he? And forgot to put his brakes on so it ran back into the verge.'

47

'And he was threatenin' them with all sorts of things if they ever came back.'

'I reckon I owe him my life.'

'So do I,' she said, and he remembered her charging in, tearing at them.

'You was brave as well,' he said.

'Were.' She put him right. 'Were brave.'

'Who was he, anyway?'

They had left the green and the houses behind them and were almost at the entrance to the lane that climbed the hill. She stopped in front of him, took a handkerchief from her skirt pocket, told him to spit on it, then began wiping blood from his cheek and the corner of his mouth.

'His name is Bob Wood,' she said. 'Haven't you seen him before?'

'Not that I know of. Should I?'

'Maybe, maybe not.' She rubbed his face. 'He comes from Stokeley.' That was the village in the next valley. 'Keep still or she'll see you've been fightin'. Does it hurt?'

'It don't bother me.'

'You shouldn't speak like that.'

'You do.'

She blushed. 'Well it's natural to me.'

He held her wrist. 'I wish you wouldn't say things like that about yourself. It makes me angry.'

'Does it!' She twisted her wrist free from his grip and rubbed at his wounds fiercely. 'Well I ain't ashamed of the way I speak, high and mighty Charlie Hoskins. But what's natural to me and what's natural to you are two different things so you might as well get used to it.' She stabbed at his cheek. 'And so might your mother.'

He stayed silent.

'That's shut you up,' she said.

He waited until she had finished rubbing his face and stood back. 'Tessa?'

'What?' She did not look at him.

48

'If you make out we're so different, how come we both know about the pond?'

'Oh, that.' She put the handkerchief back in her pocket. The fight and the bruises on his face had driven magic out of her mind.

'It happened again,' he said. 'Last night.'

He told her everything, and as he was speaking she noticed his slightly lopsided mouth. It made him pitiful. And he had sad eyes. He seemed to have put himself at her mercy, and suddenly she wanted to hurt him.

'Man wearing a cloak!' she said. 'When's your imagination going to stop running away with you, Chuck Hoskins?'

'I saw him.'

'You *thought* you did.'

Her antagonism puzzled him. He looked lost, out of his depth, and merely because she was stronger her cruelty overflowed.

'Do you know why I was down by the stream with Big Fletch? It was because I couldn't stand bein' up here with you and bein' told all that stuff about a stupid pond that makes you go little, and I felt I wasn't myself any more because I was starting to believe it! And now it's a man in a cloak in the middle of the night. Honestly, Chuck, what are you playing at? *Nothin'* happened last night, nothin' at all. You was dreaming!'

'Were,' he said.

He saw her full lips quiver, and her eyes grow luminous. Her anger was spilling over into tears as much for herself as for him. She saw him standing meekly in front of her and her heart ached, but the demon of cruelty continued to put words in her mouth. 'I think I hate you, Chuck Hoskins,' she said.

'I don't care.' His hand wanted to reach for hers, but he hesitated. 'I've still got the ring,' he said.

I saw he wasn't going to reach out all the way and touch

me—he wasn't going to hold a girl's hand no matter how much he wanted to—so it was me who snatched at his fingers and ran with him into the lane and up through the tunnel of trees. I kept ahead of him so I could bunch my hair up out of his sight and wipe my eyes with it, but we were just about up to his house before they were anything like dry and then I couldn't really turn back so I went with him through the gate and down the steps to the lawn.

I've never felt so much out in the open. I was on this green platform high over the valley with nowhere to hide and all the windows of the house peeping at me through the trees and flowers, and I was so nervous I said things he couldn't understand.

'Cushions,' I said. 'I know what the cushions were. Pink ones.'

I know it's not fair to blame him for being mystified but I was in such a hurry I said to him, 'Quick, give me the ring.' He fumbled a bit but he found it and I told him to keep watch because I wanted to try it and then get away. I hadn't quite thought out how I *was* going to get away if I did go little, but I took it and got down beside the water. I remember I didn't feel foolish, although anybody else would have thought what I was doing was pretty silly. Anybody, of course, except Chuck, and he was saying, 'Cushions? What about pink cushions?'

I had knelt down beside the pool and was dipping the ring into the water to make ripples, and at the same time I was hoping he would watch the house. I said, 'If you went tiny and got up close to somebody's hand what would it look like?'

I heard him say, 'I don't know,' and I told him, 'Well if all you saw was a fingertip you might think it was something different.'

I left him to work it out. 'Cushions,' he said. 'Pink cushions.'

I didn't notice just then that his voice was miles away because I was suddenly very close to something I was talking about. It was right in front of me, pink and shiny. My own hand, and shiny because it was wet from the pond.

'It's worked!'

I shouted it out at the top of my voice, and I just kept on talking because it was so marvellous. 'I'm about as big as a button—or I suppose I am.' I looked down at a button on my dress, and I said to myself, 'That must be unbelievably tiny. And what about those little shoes I'm wearing—just think of the workmanship!' I couldn't believe anything could be so small and so perfect and I bent down to look at the buckle. 'That's smaller than a sequin. Smaller than a pinhead even. I should think it's the size of a full-stop.'

Then I touched the hem of my dress. 'It must be stitched with spider's web,' I said, 'and ain't my fingers tiny little things! What about my hair—it's just like gossamer, all floating.' And it was true, because I shook my head and my hair was held in the air as though it lay on water.

I stood still for a moment and let it settle, but I kept on talking as though I was two people. 'The only trouble is, I seem to be about the right size—it's everything else that's gone huge. I mean that thread in my dress isn't really spider's web, is it?' I took a close look at it, and it wasn't.

But spider's web stayed in my mind. Spiders. I glanced round quickly. Nothing, thank goodness. The stone I was standing on just had humps of delicate moss, like bushes, and there were patches of yellow and green and russet red that made me feel I was in a secret garden. It was lovely. I touched the tiny little flowers of the moss and made them tremble. 'But I wish Chuck was here,' I said, and then I wondered why he wasn't.

'I expect I've got to look in a different kind of way to see if he's still normal size.' I shielded my eyes and gazed towards the horizon across the water where I'd left him.

'Is that him? That great bluish cliff must be his jeans, and up there I can make out his T-shirt and his face. Chuck!'

His head was like a great monument in the sky and I was yelling up at it, 'Chuck, I'm down here!'

Then I heard some noises high overhead, first from one side and then the other, sort of see-saw rumblings in the sky, and I realized it was voices. Somebody else was coming near.

'Chuck!'

My yell was so tiny it hardly seemed to reach the water. I saw his huge head move, but so slowly and so slightly I knew he hadn't heard me.

'Chuck!'

All the power of my lungs couldn't reach him, so I gave up. 'Oh well, I'll just have to get big again. Cushions, that's what I need, flying cushions.' And then for the first time the most peculiar thing of all came into my head. I was going to have to look for myself—my big self that should be somewhere near. I turned round quickly, and my heart was going so fast I couldn't get my breath. But it was going to be quite easy after all because my shoe was no distance away and there I was, crouching down, with one hand touching the ground. I could see my big face, tilted and looking down, but it wasn't moving and its eyes didn't seem to see anything.

'Right then, Tessa,' I said to it, 'if you're listening to yourself, tell yourself to pick yourself up.' But nothing moved. 'Very well, then, I'll have to climb up and make you do it.'

I could see her arm sloping down and she must have had the back of her hand on the stone because I could see one of her fingers quite close. But it wasn't what I expected. It was smooth just where I expected to see the ridges of her fingertips, and it was shiny and seemed to be made of overlapping segments.

I touched it. I thought that as soon as I did that I would be big again and feel just as though I was coming out of a faint. Nothing happened. So I touched it again.

There was a slight sucking sound and the segments slid

together like a telescope being shut.

'That's funny,' I said. 'It doesn't look like anything I'd call a fingertip.'

And the reason for that was it *wasn't* a fingertip. It wasn't part of me at all. I'd walked right up to an enormous earthworm and pressed its slimy side, and now its huge blind head was rearing up and coming round to get me.

10

Trapped Butterfly

It was happening again. Chuck heard voices and glanced down to Tessa kneeling at the water's edge. She seemed to have heard nothing, yet even the words were clear and he recognized the vibration of the man's voice.

'My house is so closely surrounded by trees, Mrs Hoskins, that I live in a constant twilight, which is why I am overjoyed to have found this spot high above the forest gloom.'

Chuck tried to get Tessa to her feet, but failed. 'Oh hell,' he said softly. 'Oh hell.'

The man's sleek white head came into view beyond the flowerbed, and then Chuck heard his mother. 'My son is the problem. He loves this house.'

'I sympathize, my dear lady, indeed I do. But only consider the benefits—the better schooling for him, the financial independence for you. The decision cannot be so harsh as it seems to you at the moment.'

'I've been worried about him ever since his father . . . He's too much alone up here, too cut off.'

'I'm not!' Chuck let the words leap out. 'I like it here! I want to stay!'

He silenced them. He saw their heads turn towards him, surprised, but immediately the man's wrinkles became a smile and he turned the gleam of his eyes on Chuck's mother. 'I do like your son, ma'am. If I am not mistaken, he has the cut and thrust of his father's personality. He has the dash of the warrior about him, and that must make his mother proud.'

Chuck saw Trudy's face soften. She was being told what

she wanted to hear, and the bird man pleased her even more when he went ahead of her and gallantly handed her down the steps to the lawn.

The worm's pink mouth, like the moist tip of an elephant's trunk, reached for Tessa and sent her stumbling back. She fell and was completely at its mercy as the mouth swung low, hovered over her for a long moment and then, as though it had lost interest, drifted blindly away. She scrambled to her feet, but there was no need to run, for the worm was moving away and was too slow to be frightening. The only problem was that its segmented body was a barrier between her and the great figure of herself which she had to reach.

As her panic drained away she found she was talking to herself, describing for her own benefit what she saw beyond the worm.

'Those are my shoes. And that's my feet in them, I suppose, and those must be my legs—but aren't they thick! And that's my dress.'

She looked down at her own tiny dress and swung the filmy skirt, but the great folds and heavy shadows above were as motionless as stone.

'Hey, you!'

She called out to the chin and nose and eyebrows that held themselves high against the blue sky and, like the gigantic statue of an Egyptian queen, refused to look down.

'Are you asleep up there? Are you in a dream?'

Not the slightest movement stirred the huge figure.

'Well please yourself, I'll be up there to see you in a minute.'

The worm, intent on other things, began to move past her. 'Hurry up,' she told it, 'you're getting in the way now.' But the segments took their time. 'It's just like waiting for a train to go by,' she said, and looked up and beyond herself.

High overhead there was a sound like winds gusting and clashing in the clear sky. Voices. That meant other people. Suddenly it was urgent to be up there, able to move.

Chuck glanced down at Tessa's crouching figure and knew what had happened. He took a step forward to shield her, but it was useless.

'The young lady,' said the bird man, 'has obviously found something of extraordinary interest. Have you, my dear?' He was leaning to one side to peer around Chuck, and Tessa did not stir.

'What's wrong with the girl?' said Trudy Hoskins. 'Has she gone into a trance?'

'Something like that.' Chuck did not want the man to know anything. 'We were just doing a sort of experiment. I don't want her to move for a minute.'

'But I suppose she has a tongue in her head,' said his mother. 'Can't she even speak to us?'

Chuck shook his head.

'Such a charming girl,' said the bird man. 'So pretty.'

'Maybe,' said Chuck's mother.

'I am sure I have seen her in the village.' The eyes twinkled in the long face. 'With the boys.'

'More than likely.'

Anger made Chuck desperate. 'We can't leave this house, Mum! You'd never sell it if you knew what was happening!'

She was embarrassed. 'You have got yourself into a state, Charles. I am well aware of everything that's taking place.'

'No, you're not! You wouldn't talk to me like that if you did. Like a stranger. You was Trudy to me this morning, but you ain't now—and I ain't in a state, I'm speaking the truth!'

She turned away, reddening. 'What am I to make of him, Mr Falconer?'

It was the first time Chuck had heard the man's name, and Mr Falconer appeared to be enjoying himself.

56

'Give the boy his head, dear lady. Let him explain.'

'It's all nonsense.'

He raised one of his exceptionally large hands in a gesture meant to calm her. 'What may be nonsense to you and I, Mrs Hoskins, may appear differently to the young. He is an admirable boy, your son, and I do not doubt that he is capable of seeing things that are hidden from others.' He swung back to Chuck. 'So what have you to tell us, my boy?'

The look of inquiry he turned on Chuck was so intense that it made him hesitate. The little man was too keen to know.

'Charles, we're waiting.' His mother's anger was rising.

'Somebody was here last night,' he said, all the anger gone out of his voice.

'You know very well I had a visitor.'

'Not him. Somebody else. I saw him on the lawn, dancing. He had a cloak.'

'Really!' She gave a deep sigh. 'This is getting beyond anything I've ever heard—even from you.'

'But I know who it was.' It was a guess, but he nodded towards the bird man. 'Him.'

No quiver of surprise stirred a single white hair of Mr Falconer's sleek head. Instead, the long face became serious, and the deep-set eyes gazed out at him, brown and tranquil, like an animal in hiding. Then the voice buzzed.

'Dancing, you say?'

Chuck nodded.

'Cloaked, you say?'

He nodded again.

'White-haired, you say?'

'I didn't say. I didn't notice your hair.'

The smile was slow to come and when it did it was barely noticeable. Mr Falconer simply fell silent, leaving others to draw conclusions.

'Charles, why are you saying such things?' His mother was speaking quietly. 'You know nothing happened.'

'But it did!'

'I can't stand much more of this.' She had her hands clasped tightly in front of her. 'Will you please leave us. Both of you.'

'I can't leave Tessa.'

'Take her with you!'

'Trudy.' He was pleading with her. 'She can't move.'

'Why not?'

'You know why.' He saw his mother move forward and in desperation he turned and shouted, 'Tessa!'

When the noise roared from far above, Tessa was already running. By putting her hands over her ears she had turned the gusting gales into words and knew what was happening. The worm's segments brushed the moss, rustling, and made way for her, but then, as she ran, she saw she would never reach her hand. Her huge forearm was supported on her knee, and her hand was clear of the ground. The fingers made a canopy over her head and she leapt but could not touch them.

'Chuck!' she yelled. 'Help me!'

He alone heard the tiny sound and saw her. He stooped and reached, cupping the little figure but afraid to grasp it in case he should pinch out its life.

'What are you doing?' Trudy stood above them both. 'What have you got there?'

'Nothing.' He felt Tessa clamber into his palm.

'But I can see something. What is it?'

She had come forward and was standing in front of Mr Falconer when Chuck raised his hand so that only she could see, and he opened his fingers.

'There she is!' he said. 'Tessa!'

Trudy's head drew back. 'Don't put that horrible thing near me. You know I can't stand them.'

Mr Falconer came closer. 'What have you discovered, my boy? Some creature of surpassing interest, I'll be bound.'

'A moth,' said Trudy. 'A horrible moth!'

He could feel Tessa moving like something fluttering in his hand, and suddenly he was grinning. 'Not a moth, Trudy. It's a butterfly—a really pretty one.'

But he gave her no chance to see it. He reached down as though he intended to help the kneeling Tessa to her feet, and as their hands touched he felt the tickling in his palm cease as she left him.

11
Seen from the Sky

It doesn't worry me if somebody calls me 'young man', but it makes me squirm to hear a girl called 'young lady'. It seems to turn them into something different, as if they were so fragile they mustn't be touched, especially by someone as horrible as a boy, or else it means that the person saying it just doesn't like the girl enough to call her by her proper name. Either way, I reckon it's a pretty nasty way to talk to a girl, and my mother did it when she came back after seeing the bird man off the premises and found us still on the lawn.

She looked at Tessa for a long time and then she said, 'Well that was quite a performance you gave, young lady.'

Tessa stayed quiet. You couldn't blame her. But Trudy hadn't finished.

'Just what are you trying to prove?' she said.

'Nothing,' said Tessa. 'I couldn't help it.'

'Couldn't help keeping your back to us while we were talking to you? Are you being serious, dear?'

Tessa had gone pale. She was either going to shout back, or cry. Whatever she did would just about finish everything, so I said, 'It ain't her fault.' I just about shouted it, as a matter of fact, because I reckoned it wasn't fair her getting all the nastiness when the things I'd done had been even worse. 'It was that pond,' I said. 'It does things to people.'

Then Trudy turned on me, and it was just as if she was chiselling each word into my skin. 'You're a disgrace to me, Charles Hoskins. Not only can anybody see you have been in a fight, but you bring your guttersnipe manners home with you.'

I started to say something, but she just drilled straight on. 'You can shrug that off if you like—I'm just about past caring what you get up to when you're out of my sight—but when you make up all sorts of fantastic nonsense and then you accuse Mr Falconer of creeping about on this lawn in the middle of the night it's a very different matter. Have you any idea of the damage you cause and the pain you bring on other people!'

She was so hard and angry she almost kept me quiet, but not quite. 'It *was* him,' I said. 'I know it was. I wish you'd believe some of the things I say, Trudy.'

'And I forbid you to call me Trudy.' She was really mean. 'Especially in front of other people.'

'Tessa's not other people.'

'That's a matter of opinion, Charles.'

I heard Tessa give a sort of sob, and then suddenly I was alone. They seemed to vanish. Tessa was running away in one direction, and Trudy had turned her back and was going indoors. I didn't know which one to go after so I didn't follow either of them. I just felt miserable.

All I had left was that pond, and even that was useless because clouds had come up and covered the sun and I was absolutely certain that it wouldn't work unless it could dazzle you. But I didn't even want to try. I just trailed indoors.

Trudy was in the kitchen. 'You made her cry,' I said.

She said, 'I've got a lot to do this morning so don't get under my feet.'

'You made Tessa cry.'

'Nonsense.'

'You were pretty horrible to her.'

She was washing dishes and she kept on doing it as though nothing that was going on mattered very much. All she said was, 'That's not a very nice thing to say about your own mother.'

'Tessa doesn't like you and I don't blame her.'

'Now just you listen to me!' She had her hands in the

sink but she swung round so sharp she made me jump. 'I don't know what it is that's been going on between you and that girl, but it's got right out of hand and it's got to stop. All this silliness about the pond. You've . . .' She could hardly think what to say next she was so mad. 'You've got into a strange state, the pair of you, and it's not right with people of your age. Holding hands and every-thing, I've seen you.'

'Anyway it's better than what you're doing.'

'And what do you mean by that?'

We were both red. I was so embarrassed about Tessa and me I was sweating. But I'd said too much.

'Come on, out with it.' She was furious. 'Just what are you trying to tell me?'

I couldn't say anything. I had my thoughts but I couldn't bring them out. 'Nothing,' I said.

She knew I suspected something, and she didn't like me for it. She told me to go to my room, and she went back to the dishes. I was afraid I'd started off another disaster so I tried to see her face. It wasn't any good. 'You heard me,' she said. 'Go to your room. At once!'

She didn't even bother to look at me, and that made me angry. 'You've spoiled everything!' I said, and then I told her that it wasn't only Tessa who didn't like her. I didn't, either.

I didn't give her a chance to answer. I did what she said. I went upstairs and lay on my bed and started thinking. About my dad, mainly. Ever since he died she had been different. Except just recently. She'd been a lot more cheerful, but that only made me feel worse. It wasn't right.

I was still curled up on my bed and thinking about Dad when I heard her open my door.

She called me Chuck but I didn't turn round. Then she said, 'I've got to go out again today. It's important.'

She didn't even tell me I was lying on the bed with my shoes on, so I knew she was feeling very different, but I didn't answer.

'I've left you something nice for lunch. I won't be long.'
I was still facing the wall.

'Aren't you going to say goodbye?'

I wanted to make it up, I really did, so I rolled over, but when I saw she was all dolled up, make-up and everything, I just said 'Goodbye' and wouldn't even let her touch me.

It was pretty rotten, *and* pretty childish, I know it was, but nothing seemed right. If only my dad had been there he'd have seen what was happening and he wouldn't have let us be like that. He had that funny accent, because he was foreign, and I wanted to hear him again so bad it was like an ache.

Downstairs in the kitchen just about everything I liked was all ready for me on the table, and I did eat because I was hungry, but I couldn't enjoy it because I felt stiff, as though I was waiting for something to happen.

I left the kitchen and started wandering about as though I hadn't any idea what to do, but all the time I knew exactly where I was going. The grandfather clock in the hall said it was almost noon and its tick made the whole house seem even quieter than usual. I opened the door to the sitting room in time with the tick of the clock so that it would cover the click of the door catch, and when I went in I drifted across the room quite silently, every footstep deadened by the carpet.

In the far corner, away from the window, there's a bureau with a glass-fronted bookcase above it. The brass key was in the lock of the bureau as usual and I turned it and pulled down the leaf before I opened the glass doors of the bookcase. There was a fat photograph album among the books, and I took it down and laid it on the desk. Then the house was silent again. Even turning the thick pages made no noise.

People sometimes don't believe me when I tell them that my father once stole an aeroplane, but I had proof and it was in front of me. It was a photograph, and it took up the whole of one of the black pages in the album. It showed the

63

aeroplane and the man who stole it. It was a single-seater plane, flat-nosed and a bit stubby, and my dad stood beside it, just under the cockpit. He was a bit like the plane, broad and not very tall, and he wore flying overalls with map pockets above the knees. His dark hair was fairly long, I suppose, but it was brushed down flat and shiny, and he had thick eyebrows and a black moustache. People say I have high cheekbones the same as his and I look like him when I smile, but he wasn't smiling then. In fact he looked pretty dangerous.

I knew everything about the picture, even the way the blades of grass showed up against the tyres of the undercarriage, and I looked at it for a long time. It was my dad when he was a pilot in the Hungarian Air Force, and the plane was the one he stole when he had to run away from the government. His name was Karel Horvath then, and he didn't speak any English.

I eased the photograph out of its mounts and turned it over. It had been stamped on the back with the name of a German newspaper, and there was some of my dad's handwriting which I couldn't read because even the letters weren't English, but I knew what it said. It was the date and the place in Hungary where he stole the plane, and the place he landed in Germany. He always told me he looked fierce because he was scared and thought he was going to be shot.

He was mad on planes, madder than me, madder than anybody I ever came across. There were loads of aeroplane pictures in the album, because he got a job flying, first of all in Germany, then in England. Big aeroplanes, some of them, and he used to wear uniform, but then the planes got smaller and that's when I knew him—when I got *born*, as a matter of fact. By then he was at the little airfield at Cardham just over the hill from here where he used to teach people how to fly. Me as well, more or less. He used to take me up in a glider. And Trudy. He always said she made him stay in this country. He said he didn't marry her because she was pretty or anything, but because she had the sort of name he was used to and could say. Trudy. You ought to have heard him say it—it sounded more foreign than Horvath even. But he changed that to Hoskins, because he said she'd made him into an Englishman. That made her laugh. She used to laugh a lot, and so did he.

He reckoned I was brave when he first took me flying, but I wasn't. I was scared for a long time. Even looking at photographs taken from the air made me feel giddy, but taking pictures was one of the things he liked most of all. He used to fly over people's houses and sell them the pictures. He took a lot of pictures of our house just because he liked it so much. And he'd read things about the village as well. I heard him tell Trudy once he was going to be an English gentleman, and she said the only English thing about him was that he was crazy, so he said, 'I vill start from there,' and they laughed until they were rolling about, practically.

I was crazy as well as I looked at those pictures because I began to listen for his voice. I had the idea that the house kept the echo for ever and all I had to do was pick out the sound. I could hear the tick-tock of the clock in the hall and it was saying listen, listen, listen, and I was trying to hear beyond it, to where the whispers always are, and I could pick up the sound the house seems to make as it breathes. But if there were any words they were too faint. Unless the listening was the words. If I hadn't been sitting back in my chair and listening so hard I would never have tilted my head back and my eyes, which were not looking at anything, would never have rested where they did.

What I saw was the gap on the shelf where the album belonged, and just visible was the edge of something behind the books. It was not hidden. It was a brown envelope too big to fit on the shelf any other way. I thought it was Trudy's exam certificates, because she was a nurse when she met Dad, but I pulled it out to have a look. And it wasn't what I thought.

There were some papers in it, but the main thing was a really big photograph. I hadn't seen it for ages, but I remembered it. It was a special one my dad had taken of the whole valley. He went up one morning to fly very high, and you could tell it was early by the shadows which stretched out a long way and put an outline around everything. The lanes between the hedges seemed to be cut very deep into the land, and you could see the valley like an oval hollow with dark woods along its sides. The trees hid most things on the slopes, but near the top of the picture it was easy to pick out our house. Its roof was quite long, but it was the garden jutting out from the hillside that was clearest.

The other stuff in the envelope wasn't very interesting. There were a few bits from newspapers but they were only stuff about the village, and there was a little leaflet about the church, nothing else, so I put them back.

The photograph was a tight fit and I was trying to squeeze it in with the other things when I saw that it should have been protected by a sheet of thin paper which had stuck inside. I eased the sheet out of the envelope and was folding its edges over the corner of the picture when I saw something that a few minutes later had me charging out of the house and down the hill.

12

Falcon Valley

Tessa's father was a one-man firm. He was a builder, and the yard in front of the house had piles of bricks and tiles and heaps of sand, among which Chuck could hear him whistling somewhere. Then he caught sight of Mr Barton loading a wheelbarrow into a van and went forward to help, but he wasn't needed.

'That's okay, boy, I've got her.' The barrow thudded upside down on to the floor of the van, its wheel hanging over the rear, and Mr Barton tied the door handles together with a length of rope. 'I was once done for having an insecure load,' he said. 'Never again, boy.' The face he turned towards Chuck he could have built himself. It was square and brick-red, even his mouth was the straight line between two bricks, and his cap made a flat waterproof roof. But his mouth turned up at the corners and his eyes shone steadily like two little blue-glazed windows. They missed nothing.

'By the look of you, Chuck boy,' he said, 'I'd say you'd been in the wars.'

'I tripped over.'

'Oh-ah,' he said. The twinkle in his eyes remained.

'I just caught my face on something.'

'Oh-ah.'

'It's not much. It doesn't hurt.'

'What about the other four, then? Are they enjoying their hospital food?'

'Four?'

His surprise made Tessa's father chuckle. 'Well *she* says four, but I expect she exaggerates.'

'She helped.' Chuck found himself blushing.

'In that case I pity that young bugger Fletcher.' But his smile had gone. 'And that young layabout's going to hear more about it next time I catch up with him.' He opened the cab door and the smile returned. He nodded his head towards the house. 'Go on. Find her.'

It was Tessa's mother who came to the door. She was as squarely built as her husband and just as forthright. She took one look at Chuck's puffed face and burst into laughter. 'No, don't tell me—you ran into a brick wall in the dark. Tessa!' She called up the stairs without taking her eyes from him and continued loud enough for Tessa to hear. 'Tessa, there's a wounded soldier come to see you.' Then, almost without lowering her voice, she said to him, 'Was she worth fightin' for, do you reckon?'

'Very much.'

She pulled a face at him. 'Well, you don't know her like I do. Here she comes, the sulky miss.' Tessa came reluctantly down the stairs behind her, and her mother had to persuade her out over the front step. 'There she is—my treasure.'

Tessa said, 'Shut up, Mum.'

'And don't she talk nice? I'll bet you don't say things like that to your mother.' She nudged Tessa's shoulder from behind, and grimaced at him over her head. 'I know you don't, because you're a gentleman.'

Chuck felt a blow behind the knees and a voice from near his waist yelled, 'He steal things, he do!'

His legs buckled and Tessa gave a snort of laughter as her young brother got both his hands in Chuck's hair and pulled as he yelled even louder. 'Search him, Tessa! I've got him in my vice-like grip!'

'Jago you young demon!' Mrs Barton dived at him. 'Let go!'

'He's a pincher!' bawled Jago.

Chuck eased the small fingers from his hair, and Jago was dragged away and the door shut.

'Serves you right,' said Tessa.

'What have I done?'

'You shouldn't be such a snob.'

He had to follow her around to the chicken run at the back of the house before he caught up with her. 'I've been finding out things,' he said, 'and I'm not a snob.'

'Who said you were?'

'You did.'

'No I never! Anyway I didn't mean it.'

He knew his mouth was open and his brain wasn't working fast enough.

'You look stupid,' she said.

'I've been looking through some things that belonged to my dad.' It was unfair to mention his father, but it worked. She was listening. 'It's got something to do with the pond. You've got to come and look.'

Eyes that were as blue as her father's gazed at him for a long moment before she replied, and he could see the pain and anger struggling in her face. 'How can you ask me to go back to your house, Chuck Hoskins, when your mum treats me like that? I ain't . . . I'm not . . .' She corrected herself and then despised herself for doing it. 'I ain't going to have her talk to me like that again, not ever!'

'She won't. She ain't there.'

'It don't matter. And stop imitating me!'

'I ain't. I'm not. Oh hell.'

She saw his head droop, his battered face bewildered, and the thought of Jago's attack just a moment ago made her bite her lip to stop laughing. 'Poor old Chuck,' she said. 'Everybody's got it in for you, ain't they?'

He looked up, still glum, and solemnly put her right. 'Haven't they,' he said.

'You beast! And I thought you was trying to be nice to me.' She took a mock slap at him and so nearly connected with the grin on his wounded face that he backed away. She went after him. 'If I just get my hands on you, Chuck Hoskins . . .'

'You'll have to do it in my house.' He grabbed her by the wrist and ran with her, tugging her up the lane all the way to his door.

She allowed herself to be led into a room she had never seen before, and the house closed around her. The slow beat of the clock in the hall seemed to be footsteps coming closer, and she was holding her breath when Chuck took her to the desk in the far corner and lifted the sheet of paper that covered a large photograph.

'Recognize it?' he asked, but she shook her head, barely glancing at it. 'Don't worry,' he said, 'there's nobody here but us, and I'll make sure we're not caught.'

In spite of that she was crushing the fingers of his hand as she forced herself to take in the photograph. Now she saw the village and the place by the stream where they had had the fight, and further downstream the bridge where the valley levelled out and the land was marshy. 'Jessie's Bridge,' she said, and then she went back upstream seeking her own house. 'You can only see our roof.' She was disappointed. 'I didn't know we were so deep in the woods.' But the garden and lawn where he lived were quite clear.

Chuck stood back. 'Does it remind you of anything? I know it's the village, but does it remind you of anything else? Look.'

He let the covering sheet fall back into place, and she saw that a picture had been drawn on it. It was a large bird, perched on a branch, and it filled the sheet. It had a hooked beak and claws. 'It looks like a hawk to me,' she said.

'Anything else?'

'What else is there?' It wasn't even a very good drawing. 'There's quite a lot of squiggles,' she said.

'Let go of my fingers, Tessa.' He eased his hand free, and she realized how hard she had been gripping. He leant forward and with both hands smoothed the paper so that the photograph could be seen through it. 'Now do you see?'

She stooped over it alongside him. 'It looks a bit like a tracing,' she said.

'It is. It's a map.'

'But it's a bird as well.' She looked closer. 'It's got its claws on Jessie's Bridge, and the road is the branch. What's that bit of shading on its wing?' She folded the sheet back and discovered that the dark patch of its wing feathers was the woods on the hillside. 'They fit just about perfectly.'

'Everything does. Look.' He drew his finger around the outline of the hawk's head on the sheet and then on the photograph.

They stood back. It was quite clear. Even without half closing their eyes the shape of the bird was obvious. The valley was a huge hawk.

'And the eye.' He pointed. 'Look at the eye, Tessa.'

It had the fierce frown of a falcon. She stooped to see its detail. The dark line above it was the thatched roof of the house that enclosed her now. And the eye, the staring semi-circle below it, was the lawn.

'It's us!' Chuck had been holding in his excitement, but now he was feverishly spilling papers from the big envelope. 'We're right in the hawk's eye. And there's more!'

It was then that she heard a sound. The garden gate clicked. 'Listen!' Voices reached them from outside and she ceased to breathe. 'It's your mother!'

He listened. Footsteps on the stone terrace outside. 'We can't get out,' he said.

He was far too calm. She held her clenched hands close to her face, horrified to see him smile and even pause to push the papers into the bureau and close the flap. His puffed cheek made his grin even more lopsided and infuriating.

'We'll have to hide,' he said, and let her go ahead of him across the room and into the hall. 'Now upstairs.' She trembled so much she almost missed her footing, and on the landing she was ready to panic and run but he led her to a door and opened it. 'My room,' he said, and she went

71

ahead of him while he stood in the doorway, listening.

'Is it?' she whispered. 'Is it your mother?'

She longed for him to deny it, but he nodded. 'They're staying outside,' he said, 'I wish I could see them.'

She stood in the middle of the room, hugging her arms close to her body and biting her lip. 'How am I going to get out, Chuck?'

'Don't worry.' He stepped on to his bed and opened the window. She saw him put his foot on a shelf and climb higher, and she could bear it no longer. She tugged at his foot.

'Come back, Chuck, I don't like it!'

He turned to speak over his shoulder. 'The bird man's with her. Come and take a look.'

'No!'

'You might as well. We can't get out.' He was enjoying himself.

'I hate you, Chuck Hoskins! I really do!'

'Come on.' He reached down to help her up. 'We might find out something.'

'So will they if they look this way.'

'They won't. They're far too busy.'

She climbed alongside him. 'I can hardly move.' The window was so small they were squeezed together, but as she gazed out she realized they had little to fear. The tall flowers at the edge of the terrace were a screen and the voices were coming from beyond it.

'Where are they?' she asked, and as if they had heard her, two figures moved out on to the lawn. There was the white hair of Mr Falconer alongside Chuck's mother. Their backs were towards the house, and Tessa breathed again.

'Can we creep out while they're down there?' she said. 'Can we?'

'Hang on a minute. I'm trying to hear what they're saying.'

But it was useless. They were too far away, and then the bird man stooped and was almost out of sight.

72

'Damn!' said Chuck.

It was the last word Tessa heard. She saw the man's white head dip down, and the pond become visible just beyond it. And then she saw him reach and dabble his fingers so that the water sparkled in the sun. And then nothing.

13
Another Country

There was nothing to clutch at—no window ledge or thatch. Tessa was falling free, tumbling over and over as she sailed down through what appeared to be a gigantic room. Walls were far away and rose from deep shadows as though night itself was somewhere down there, far below, and as she turned, riding the air, she saw nothing above her but the distant ceiling and the great paper globe of a lampshade, big enough to contain a circus. It drifted higher, and then she was head down and sliding past a shelf of huge books with their titles printed in letters as large as herself. But they were out of reach and winking by like windows in a skyscraper.

Suddenly, out of dimness, she plunged into a shaft of sunlight. Motes of dust sparkled like stars, and through them she saw another falling figure, twisting in a swirl of golden particles.

'Chuck!'

She shouted his name, but before she could tell whether or not he had heard, she slid out of the light and lost sight of him.

Below her a sea of white mist was rising, humped and hollowed against the darkness as though it had risen in the night and she was falling out of the room into a cloud. She spread her arms and legs to clutch at the whiteness as it rushed nearer and folded over her.

Chuck, plunging through sunlight, heard his name and twisted. The sudden movement did nothing but send him into a spin and he was still trying to control it, tumbling and diving and tumbling again, when a pale hillock rose from the dimness and he hit it. He felt the smack of a coarse surface, and then the hillock, like a puffball, collapsed beneath him.

He lay on his back in a deep indentation and gently moved all his joints.

'At least I'm not hurt.' He spoke the words aloud to calm himself and then, finding that his voice was deadened by the collapsed hillock and there seemed no danger of being overheard, he added, 'but I've been taken by surprise again.'

He got cautiously to his feet. Whiteness lay all around him. It could have been the North Pole. 'Except,' he said, 'it's not cold, and this isn't snow.' The white surface seemed to be a woven carpet, and he was stooping to examine it more closely when, once more, he heard his name.

'Chuck!' Tessa was coming towards him across the white plain, stumbling where ridges lay across her path. 'We're in another country!' In whichever direction she looked the plain ended in snowy mountains. 'Where are we?'

He already knew. It was a different question that was on his mind.

'Tessa,' he said, 'you know what's happened, don't you?'

She was still gazing at the white landscape, bewildered. She shook her head.

'It's the first time we've both been small at the same time,' he said. 'And we weren't even beside the pond.'

He thought she was never going to look his way, and when she did turn towards him it was only to deepen the mystery. 'And it couldn't have been my silver ring,' she said. 'It's still on my finger.'

'So it's the pond that does it.' Chuck was speaking to himself, almost ignoring her. 'Ever since that chain fell into it. That's what started it. And now we've only got to see the sun or the moon in it and this happens.' He looked up.

'But why us, Tess? Why doesn't it happen to anybody else?'

She twisted the tiny silver ring on her finger. It must have been no more than the thickness of a thread but it gleamed like silver water. Like water. And suddenly she understood. 'How did we make the water sparkle the first time?'

'We made it ripple.'

'How?'

'With our hands, of course. We splashed it about.'

'Yes?' She was leaning forward, expecting him to see what she already knew, but he was slow to make the connection. 'We dipped our fingers into the water, Chuck. It wet us. We were baptized!'

Then it dawned on him. 'And it has happened to nobody else,' he said. 'Nobody. That's why nobody believes.' In the midst of the whiteness he started to dance. 'Tessa, you're brilliant!'

'But I still don't know where we are.'

'That's easy.' He stopped dancing and tilted his head back to look upwards and get his bearings. He could see books on high shelves, an aeroplane bigger than any airliner and motionless in space, and the great highway of sunshine through which he had plunged. He shielded his eyes and saw the threads which held the model aeroplane in mid-air, but the glare of sunlight prevented him focusing on the window through which it slanted.

'We're in my room,' he said.

'Whereabouts?' She couldn't make it out.

'On my bed.'

'It doesn't seem like a bed to me.'

'I forgot to make it. The sheet's a bit crumpled up.'

She opened her eyes wide at the white mountains. 'More than a bit.'

'Well I couldn't help it. I didn't have time.'

'And look at you now.' She was laughing. 'You couldn't lift a single sheet, not even a corner. Still, I suppose you

76

could always sleep in a matchbox.'

He was about to answer when a sound from far away silenced him. There was a creak and a dull thud, and then a noise like the murmur of waves breaking on a beach. Tessa recognized it before he did.

'It's your mum,' she said. 'She's brought him into the house. They're talking.'

He nodded. The creak and thud had been the door downstairs. 'But I can't hear a word,' he said. 'Do you think our ears are different when we're this size?'

'Yes,' said Tessa, 'they're smaller.'

He groaned. 'I sometimes wish I was with someone with a bit more sense.'

'And I wish I was with someone who could make his own bed.'

He was listening to the sound of the distant voices. 'I bet they're talking about this house.' The indistinct rise and fall told him nothing. 'I wish I could hear.'

'Well,' she said, 'you're just the right size for getting close.'

'Tessa Barton is not only very beautiful,' he said, 'she's a genius.' He turned and began to move away, but pulled up sharply. 'Except for one thing—how are we going to get off this bed?'

'Easy.' She ran past him towards the edge and jumped. 'Tessa!'

He couldn't prevent the cry that jerked from him as she vanished, and he lunged forward. But she had not plunged headlong into space. The sheet of his unmade bed lay in a long curve to the floor and she was already far below, tobogganing down.

He sat and launched himself after her. The fuzzy surface of the sheet made a track as slippery as packed snow, and the first vertical drop was eased by the gentle pressure as the curve pressed into his back and smoothed his way to the tumbled wrinkles at the foot of the slope.

'Just for once,' she said, 'I'm glad you're so messy your

room's a heap.'

'Good job we're not in yours, then.'

'You don't know anything about me.'

'I know one thing.'

'What's that?'

'You talk like a girl.'

'Well I am a girl. What's wrong with that?'

'Nothing.'

'Glad to hear it.'

They were clambering over the tilted ice floes of the wrinkled sheet as they spoke.

'On the other hand,' said Tessa, 'there's a lot wrong with being a boy.'

'What, for instance?'

'General stupidity,' she said. 'Childishness. Always wanting to be the best at everything.'

'Is that all?'

'That'll have to do for now. I'll tell you more later.'

'Thank you very much!'

'Don't mention it.' She looked at him slyly, along her eyes. 'I mean it,' she said. 'Boys are like that, and you're one of them.'

He stumbled forward a few steps before he replied, then he said, 'I understand everything a lot better now, Tessa. You've opened my eyes, because I used to think you were very pretty, but now you've told me I'm stupid so I reckon I must be wrong.'

'Pig,' she said.

They fell silent as they stepped on to the bare floor-boards and walked towards the door. It was shut, but that was no problem to them. The gap beneath it was so great they could only just reach up and touch the bottom edge. It was a door as old as the house and its massive timbers had cracks into which they could have thrust an arm.

He stood looking at it. 'Just think,' he said, 'I can move all that with one hand.'

'Not now, you can't.' She reached for the hand that he

had lifted to press experimentally against the woodwork and tugged him forward. 'We haven't time to daydream.'

Under the false ceiling made by the bottom of the door, the landing at the stairhead opened into the vast space of the hall. They clambered on to the carpet and sank waist deep into its pile as they stumbled through it to where the banisters marched up the stairs from far below and were spaced along the landing like the columns of a temple. Beyond them, without any railing for people of their size, there was a drop into nothingness.

Voices boomed from the space beneath. They could feel the air tremble against their cheeks, but the vibration swamped the words until they sat at the base of one of the columns and cut down the noise by putting their hands over their ears.

It was the man they heard first. He was saying:

'. . . and I am sure you will never regret it, Mrs Hoskins.'

Then Chuck heard his mother's voice replace the rasp of the bird man.

'It's not myself I'm worried about,' she said.

'Of course not, dear lady, but your son is a boy of infinite resource, and I am quite sure he will adapt easily to a new life with new friends, new interests—new horizons will open for him!'

'I hope so.' She sounded anxious. 'But it *is* his home.'

They heard the man's wheezy chuckle. 'But you have other news, I believe, that should make him happy.'

'Please!' She hushed him. 'He may be upstairs.'

She called Chuck's name, and when there was no reply they heard her say, 'Thank goodness for that. He's outside somewhere.'

The chuckle came again. 'You have no need to distress yourself, Mrs Hoskins. He is a mature and sensible young man.'

Chuck saw Tessa put out her tongue at him, but then looked down to see the white hair moving towards the door ahead of his mother's black curls.

'There is just one small favour I would ask, Mrs Hoskins.' They paused with the door ajar. 'As I intend to build a summerhouse to overlook the valley, would you permit me to make an examination of the lawn? That rainwater pond could mean a problem with the foundations.'

His mother's reply was indistinct, but she must have agreed for he said, 'Of course, and I will choose a time that will cause you no inconvenience.'

It was then that something moved in Chuck's bedroom, and his mother called out again, 'Charles, are you there?'

She paused, listening, and now there was a danger she would climb the stairs to investigate. They did not wait to find out. They made a dash back to his room, and as soon as they ran under the door they saw what had happened. Tessa's bigger self was still at the window, looking out, but he had slid down and was now sprawled half on and half off the bed.

There were sounds down in the hall. Chuck ran to where he lay at an angle, one huge arm stretched along the floor. He scrambled into his hand, found himself being instantly lifted, rising up without effort, and the next moment he was pressing down hard with his hand on the floor and levering himself, his proper self again, upright on his bed.

He heard his mother downstairs ushering Mr Falconer out.

'Tessa!' he called softly, but she had not had time to reach herself, and gazed motionless out of the window. He turned and looked down. 'Where are you?'

He could not see her on the floor, and dared not move in case he crushed her.

'Tessa!'

A tiny voice reached him and he saw her. She was trying to climb the white slope but slipping and falling back. He stooped and let her climb on to his hand.

'Quick!' Her voice was no more than the chink of a coin, and he reached up and tipped her into her own hand, just as footsteps came up the stairs.

14
Chuck in the Dark

It was terrible—just like one of those dreams where you've got no clothes on, or the lavatory door won't shut. But it was worse because I woke up in the middle of it and it was true. I was standing on Chuck's bed and I could hear his mother on the landing just outside the door!

I haven't ever fainted but I thought I was going to. I was even sort of sinking down, trying to go small again by just shrinking away, when Chuck grabbed hold of me and dragged me across to his wardrobe. He tossed me inside like an old jacket or something, and when he slammed the door I felt like pushing it back against him in spite of everything, but it must have been just as bad for him. And it was a good job I didn't because the next thing I heard was his mother.

'How long have you been there? Didn't you hear me call?'

She sounded so much like my mum it was incredible. Then I heard Chuck tell a lie, and that was just like me sometimes.

'No,' he said, 'I didn't hear a thing.'

'Well I did. Twice. Just what have you been up to?'

She was really getting on at him, and I was squeezed among his clothes and just waiting for the pile of shoes I stood on to collapse. He's pretty untidy, is Chuck. She asked him again what he'd been doing—she was really suspicious—and instead of him saying nothing, he made it worse.

'I've just been doing the usual things,' he said. 'Going small.'

It was absolutely silent in that room. I couldn't see and I couldn't breathe, but I knew what his mother's face was like. She's ever so pretty, usually, but not so much when she's being mean.

'Charles,' she said, 'you're not persisting with that nonsense, are you?'

'But it's true. Ask Tessa.'

He did—he really did say that, and I was pushing the shoulder of one of his jackets into my mouth I was so scared. I heard him start to say something else, but he didn't get a chance.

'It's gone way beyond a joke, Charles. It's getting out of hand. You and that girl have got to stop seeing each other—I mean it. It's doing neither of you any good. You're just encouraging each other and making it worse.'

'Well it's better that than what you're doing—seeing that man.'

'What man?' All of a sudden his mother's voice changed. She was worried. 'What man do you mean?'

He'd caught her out. It was so obvious—well it was to me, but he didn't get it. Poor old Chuck, and he thought he was being so clever. Well he might have been, in a way, because when she asked him again who was it he was talking about, he said, 'The man who wants to buy this house. What man did you think I meant?'

It was right then that I began to feel I was safe, even though everything had gone very quiet again.

'Chuck'—she even called him that—'come downstairs, I want to talk to you.'

I could hear him trying not to sound cocky when he said, 'Oh, all right,' because he'd saved me from being caught. The trouble is he gets reckless. He came right close to the door and said very loud, 'Then I've got to go down to the village and see somebody on the green.' And if that wasn't bad enough he practically shouted when he got to the door, 'In about ten minutes!'

I heard him thump down the stairs, making a lot of noise just for my benefit, and I waited until I heard a door close downstairs before I came out—or tried to. There was no handle inside the wardrobe and I had to push until something gave way, and then I couldn't shut it again, so I was pretty flustered, but I was really quiet on the landing and I kept to the edge of the stairs where they wouldn't creak so much.

The hall was very warm and so full of sunlight I seemed to be wrapped in it, and I glided very quietly past the door where the voices were, and out through the kitchen to the gravel patch near his garage. Then I ran.

It's funny what you want to do after something like that. I was just longing to tell somebody—everybody, and there was the village down below all cupped in green and full of sunlight as yellow as butter and nothing was moving. Well, as a matter of fact, there was one thing moving and that was Josie Jones who came out of her gate, but she was only going as far as Strutt's shop to get something for her mother, and there was nobody else in sight.

It was a crazy sort of conversation we had. 'That's the trouble with holiday-time,' she said just as if she knew what I was thinking, 'there's nobody about. They've all gone away, I reckon, except me. And you.'

I could've said we never did go away at that time of the year because it was a busy time for my dad, with the weather letting him get on with outside jobs, but what I did say was, 'I don't want to go anywhere.'

She doesn't miss much, so she gave me a look. 'I'm not surprised,' she said. 'You've got a good reason for staying, ain't you?'

'What do you mean?' I said, as if I didn't know what was in her mind.

'You know what I mean. Him up the hill. He's still around, ain't he?'

And then she said, 'That made you go red, didn't it?' and I said, 'You want to be quiet, you do, or I'll say some things about you, Josie Jones.' But it was a waste of time, because she'd gone into the shop.

All it did was put me more on edge and I sat down on the bench on the green and began talking to myself, which I do quite a lot because it seems to give you another point of view, even though some people might think you're going mad. The hills seemed to be drowsy and the silence was rolling down off them, so even when I saw an old man tapping along to the pub I couldn't hear him and I kept saying things about Chuck. Like: 'He's a bit crazy I reckon, but I like him better than anybody else around here. I like him a lot, as a matter of fact. A lot. But his mum don't like me a bit. Anyway who does she think she is? She only comes from Stokeley and she wasn't anybody until she got married. That's what my Gran say.'

'What does she say, your Gran?'

That was Chuck right behind me. I nearly jumped out of my skin. 'None of your business,' I told him. 'And you want to be careful creeping up on people like that because you might hear something you wish you hadn't.'

That didn't bother him. He dumped himself down beside me and said, 'I just have. She's told me she's going to sell our house. To him.'

Then it was funny because he pointed over to the pub but all I could see was the old man, and Chuck said, 'No, not him. I mean that's his name on the pub, Falconer—the Falconer's Arms. And it probably belongs to him as well, because he owns Creance Hall, that's all.'

Well I knew that. I thought everybody knew Mr Falconer had come to live in the hall across the valley after his aunt died. But Chuck didn't know it—he just doesn't know anything sometimes. He kept going on about how Mr Falconer practically owned the whole valley anyway, so why should he want to buy another house—unless he knew something special, like we did.

Any minute he was going to say we should have another go at telling somebody about the pond, and that was just about the last thing I wanted to do, so I said, 'Where will you go to live, Chuck?'

That was a bit mean, really, because I knew where he'd have to go or I thought I did, but the way he sometimes can't see things that are obvious makes me impatient. He just shrugged and said, 'I don't know where we're going to go. She was going to tell me but I wouldn't let her. I left.'

Ran away, more like, and I was thinking of telling him what I knew when something very strange happened. Well two things, really, and if that didn't make everything obvious I don't know what would.

The first thing was a Land-Rover stopped in front of the pub and a man got out. I recognized him straight away but Chuck didn't. It was Bob Wood, who rescued us down by the stream. He's a chunky sort of man, quite old, but he's got a nice smile, well I think so, but to see the way Chuck was glaring at him you'd think he was an enemy. He still had Mr Falconer on his mind, that was why, but Bob Wood was really nice. He said, 'I see you've still got the scars of battle, Charles.'

'Chuck,' said Chuck.

'Sorry, I forgot. But you were doin' all right, Chuck. You both were, until I come and broke it up.'

Then the second thing happened. I don't know why I did it, but I looked away from Bob Wood just then. Maybe I'd seen his smile go a bit different. Anyway, I looked over my shoulder across the green and what I saw made me dig my nails into Chuck's arm so hard he gave a shout and said, 'What's up?'

All I had to do was nod where I was looking, and when he saw his mother he hauled me to my feet and we just flew.

15

The Quelling Eye

They dashed across the road, and Tessa dragged him around the corner of the Falconer's Arms and into the inn yard.

'This is a stupid place,' said Chuck. 'We're trapped.'

'No we ain't.' She ran ahead of him across the yard to a tiny cottage squeezed among the inn buildings. It had a whitewashed front and faced the full glare of the sun with its door open as though gasping in the heat. She plunged straight inside. 'Come on!'

He hesitated until she stepped out and pulled him into the coolness of a cramped little room. Chuck, hemmed in by furniture, could hardly move.

'We're in for it now,' he said. 'They'll think we want to pinch something.'

'Just be quiet for a minute, Chuck Hoskins.' She stood listening and then, apparently satisfied with whatever it was she had heard, she went to a low door that was placed at an angle across a corner near the fireplace. She opened it and called through, 'Gran, are you there?'

'You might've told me this was your granny's house,' he said.

'And you might've known if you wasn't so stuck up.'

'I ain't stuck up!'

'Well you act like it with your head full of stuff. You never notice nothin' that's going on around you.'

'Yes I do!'

'No you don't.'

'And,' said a sharp voice from the corner, 'I'll throw the pair of you out if you don't stop squabbling like a couple of fighting cocks. Cackle, cackle, cackle. What do you think this is, a chicken run?'

Such a small house needed a small woman, and Tessa's grandmother was barely bigger than either of them. Her small, round glasses shone like silver coins, her grey hair was cut short, except where it curled up in a little tail at the back of her head, and she came scuttling forward with her elbows out like a battling grey bantam.

'You!' She grabbed Chuck by both elbows and jerked and jostled him to a chair and pushed him into it. 'And you, my lady . . .' she dumped Tessa into a chair at the other side of the empty fireplace '. . . you put your bottom down there and don't say a word.' She stood between them, thrusting out her thin chin with her mouth pulled down grimly at the corners, and cocked her head, listening. 'That's better. Can't hear a sound now, but I was sure I heard a fox in the barnyard.'

Tessa unwisely opened her mouth.

'And you can save your breath to cool your porridge. I know who he is and where he comes from. And who his Ma is, and who she's talking to this very minute, I wouldn't be surprised. And where.' She sniffed. 'Old I may be, and old-fashioned with it, but I still know it ain't right for a young woman to go into public houses in the middle of the day.' She glared at Chuck. 'Now then, Charles Hoskins, one lump or two?' Now it was his turn to open his mouth, but before any words came she had switched her attention back to Tessa. 'What do he think he's doing, catching flies?'

'He takes two sugars, Gran. Same as me.'

'Why don't he speak up, then? He had plenty to say for hisself just a minute gone,' and she turned her back and bobbed out through the corner door. The door clapped shut and it was as though they had been watching a figure in a mechanical clock.

'You'll never get away from my Gran without having a cup of tea,' Tessa whispered, leaning towards him, 'and a biscuit.'

87

'Chocolate fingers!' She'd swung back into the room and clattered a gaudy little tin on to the table beside him. 'All boys like chocolate fingers. Don't stint yourself.' She was gone and back again with the tea tray without drawing breath. 'Have another one. I hear your mother's selling up. Where shall you live when that happens?'

'I don't know.' She was moving too fast for Chuck.

'She ought never to let it go to that stupid Falconer man.' She poured tea, and her voice rattled like a teaspoon. 'I remember him when he was a boy and he came here to have his holidays with his auntie. That's the one who's just died.' She glanced sharply at each of them. 'But you know that. And he haven't changed a bit except for his white hair. Peregrine Falconer!' She gave a snort. 'What sort of name's that to go to bed with?'

Rattle. Rattle.

'But pots o' money, I'll grant you that. More money than sense. The sort of tales he used to come out with you'd never credit. One time he reckoned he could fly. He said all the Falconers could when the conditions was right, but they never was. Hardly likely, is it? But he was that cocky he acted just as if his family still owned the valley like they used to do.' She tilted her head so Chuck was looking at a reflection of himself in her glasses. 'I suppose your head's stuffed full of nonsense as well. You wouldn't be a boy if it wasn't.'

'I was wondering,' said Chuck, 'if they ever had been able to fly.'

'What did I tell you!' The glasses flashed at Tessa. 'Boys are so stupid you can tell them anything and they believe it. It's a good job they've got us women around, ain't it?'

'Yes.' Tessa sipped her tea delicately, gazing at him over the rim of her cup. 'Boys have very simple minds.'

Chuck, meaning only to tease her, proved it. 'I can tell you something about Tessa,' he said. 'She thinks she can go small, about as big as a paper clip.'

'No I don't!' And then she mouthed more words at him

to tell him to say no more, but her grandmother missed nothing.

'Girls is used to going small. They got to pretend to because of you men.'

'That's not what I meant,' he said. 'I'm just the same as her.'

'Then you're the first man that ever admitted it, unless things have changed a lot from my young days.'

'They have,' said Tessa, and grimaced at Chuck, but her grandmother did not stop.

'And some of the small ones are the worst. Even that little Perry Falconer used to say he could quell anybody with his eye. Silly little sugar lump, him and his white hair. Old age ain't improved him one bit since the days when he used to reckon the Falconers could do anything. I'll show you something now.'

She was on her feet as she spoke, bustling towards a rack of shelves in the corner and taking down a pamphlet to show to Chuck. 'See that? History of the church, that is.'

Chuck drew in his breath sharply, surprised to recognize it. He had been looking at the same pamphlet only an hour ago, among his father's papers. She saw his surprise and waited for him to say something but he shook his head.

'Well anyway . . .' she leafed over a page '. . . just listen to what it say here about them Falconers and their nonsense.' She pushed her spectacles further up her nose and began to read. *The Falconer family, who once owned the entire valley of the Goss Beck, were commonly believed to possess the power of the Quelling Eye and could conquer their foes with a glance. Indeed, village folk were convinced that the brass hawk in the coat of arms on the family's tomb had itself the power of the Quelling Eye, and they also believed that at the time of the full moon it could take wing and snatch up people like beetles.*

Her glasses sparkled with indignation. 'Village folk! I ain't *village folk*; I'm *people* same as whoever wrote this old squit—and I'll tell you something else,' the sparkle switched suddenly to laughter, 'that old brass bird ain't there no more. That's "taken wing", I reckon.' She folded back the page and handed the pamphlet to Chuck. 'But there's a picture of it before it flew away.'

Tessa moved so that she could also see the drawing. 'I've seen that before,' she said. 'It's the same as the sign on the pub.'

'Of course it is,' said her grandmother. 'Them Falconers had their mark on everything round here, didn't they?'

Tessa suddenly crouched down beside his chair. 'And Chuck,' her voice was excited, 'it's exactly the same as that tracing your dad made!'

She looked into his face but he said nothing.

'Chuck!'

His mouth remained tight closed.

'Cat's got his tongue,' said her grandmother, and she rattled the biscuit tin under his nose. 'Have a chocolate finger, Charles Hoskins, that old bird ain't going to snaffle you up just yet.'

16

The Night Garden

Chuck had a lot to do before it got dark. At the back of the garage where his father's fishing rods still hung on the wall he found the tackle box and opened it. Everything inside lay as his father had left it, the little compartments with hooks and weights, the tray of floats banded in bright colours, everything neat and in order. It was like opening a diary and reading secret words, and if he moved anything he would dust away the last trace of his father's touch. But it was necessary. He took out a spool of fine fishing line. Then he went to the workbench where he found a tin of nails, put a few in his pocket, and took a hammer from among the tools.

In his room he managed to hammer a nail into his window ledge without his mother coming to investigate, then he tied one end of the line to it and, leaning out of the window, let the spool fall to the ground. He went down to where the spool lay on the flagstones and paid out the line, which was the finest filament he could find, as he crossed the garden to an apple tree at the corner of the lawn. He climbed the tree, easing the filament through the leaves, and secured it to another nail. Then he unwound enough line to reach the ground, cut it and looped the loose end around the nail and out of sight.

He climbed down and looked up. The line was almost invisible against the blue sky, and when a cloud drifted over and hid the sun it vanished completely.

'Good,' he said aloud, and at that moment another thought crossed his mind. 'But now there's no sun!' He turned his back on the house to take in the whole sky over the valley. The clouds were high, but thickening, and the pool reflected nothing but greyness. 'That's okay for now,' he said, 'but what about tonight if there's no moon?'

'Well what about it?' The voice from directly behind him jerked him round. His mother stood on the terrace, smiling because she had surprised him.

'You made me jump!'

'What's all this about the moon? You're not thinking of going out tonight, are you?'

'No, Trudy. Are you?'

'Mind your own business.' She was in a good humour. She must have seen him with Tessa at lunchtime running across the green but she had not mentioned it. 'You want to know more than is good for you, Chuck Hoskins.'

'Well, are you going out tonight?'

'I am, as a matter of fact.'

'You're blushing,' he said.

'Saucy little devil!' She ran down the steps. 'Just let me catch hold of you, I'll give you blush.'

He made sure the chase was away from the tree and the tell-tale line, and allowed himself to be cornered in the hall. The struggle ended with them both sitting on the floor, panting.

'Let that be a lesson to you,' she said.

'Trudy, I want to know something.'

'What's that?' She was trying to get her breath.

'You're very frisky these days,' he said. 'What's got into you?'

'Nothing that I know of. What are you getting at?'

'You just seem to be a lot happier, that's all.'

'What's wrong with that? You don't want me to mope all the time, do you? Or do you?'

'You're happy because you're going to sell this house.'

They faced each other, neither of them smiling. 'Oh Chuck,' she said softly, 'will it make you sad?'

'I don't want to leave. Not now. Not just at this minute.'

'Why?' Her face was troubled. 'What's so special about now?'

'Because . . .' He had to pause to gain courage. Her mood could change very quickly. 'Because there's something magic happening.'

She was examining him closely again, but the anger he expected did not come. 'There's no need to screw your eyes up like that,' she said. 'I'm not going to bite you. Of course there's something magic happening, absolutely magic, but I'm not going to tell you about it.'

'But . . .'

'No buts. You'll know about it all in good time. Now why don't you stop mooching around this house and go out and find your friends?'

'They've all gone on holiday.'

'There must be somebody.'

'There is, but you don't like her.'

She sighed and was about to speak but he gave her no chance. He dashed upstairs to his room, and she did not follow.

He shut his door, listening. He still had things to do and could not afford to be disturbed. When he was sure all was silent below, he took a wire paper clip from his desk and went to the window where he slipped it over the fishing line, made sure it could slide freely and laid it, still hooked over the line, on the ledge next to the nail. He had stolen a pincushion from Trudy's workbasket, and he selected the two smallest and sharpest pins he could find and put them alongside the paper clip.

Later, lying in bed, he heard a car come up the lane, and he knew his preparations had been necessary.

Tessa lay listening to night sounds. It would soon be time to creep out of the house and climb the lane to meet him, but she did not want to go. It was Chuck's idea. He was crazy to even think of it, and she was just as mad to agree.

'I don't mind being crazy.' She twisted her head so that she was whispering into her pillow. 'But you've got it wrong, Chuck.'

It was her grandmother's fault for filling his head with more stories about the Falconer family, particularly the brass bird that was supposed to fly from the Falconer tomb. He had insisted that they should go to the church to see the tomb even though they knew that the brass falcon had long since gone and all that remained was its outline in the stone and the holes made by the studs that had held it in place. But it had all made Chuck's mind race ahead so that he was convinced something was on the verge of happening, and as it couldn't any longer be in the church because the bird had flown from there, it was going to be in some other powerful place—such as his lawn, at midnight.

'But it won't work, Chuck!' Her lips made her pillow wet as she pressed it into her face. There wasn't even a full moon. He was wrong, wrong, wrong.

And then the alarm on Jago's watch, which she had stolen from his bedside, beeped in her ear. It was time to go.

She dressed quickly but did not put her shoes on until she had eased the back door shut and was outside. She listened as she knelt to tie her laces. High overhead, clouds closed soft fists over the moon and the shadows deepened under the trees, but not a leaf stirred, and by the time the clouds unclenched she was in the lane and moving through the dim dapple of the moonlight.

The car, squatting in the shadows where the lane ended, took her by surprise. She froze, standing where she was in the middle of the track, ready to turn and flee downhill. And then she breathed again. There was nobody in the car, but it did mean there was somebody else at his house.

She let out her breath angrily. 'Why didn't he tell me?'

She was on the point of turning back when the shadows closed in once more and gave her the chance to brush past the car and push open the garden gate. Chinks of light showed through the curtains of one downstairs room and she glided by, treading as softly as mist, and went down to the lawn where she vanished under the branches of the apple tree.

Through the leaves she could see the lower half of his window, but nothing more. He was probably fast asleep. It was ridiculous to be here.

The moonlight bloomed again and she turned her head. What she saw stopped her breathing. The lawn was no longer vacant.

A figure stood there. It was man-shape, but not a man. It stood upright, utterly still, and its rounded dome of a head faced her.

No air stirred in Tessa's open mouth, and no flicker of movement showed any features in the dark head. Yet it had eyes. They were invisible but she could feel them searching and, when a sound came from the house, the head dipped and swung.

Chuck eased open his window. He had tied a sheet to the leg of his bed and, as he leaned out, he held a corner of it. Whatever else happened, this time he must not go sliding down the thatch.

Below him, the night garden was motionless. The apple tree was no more than a dark mound and he was sifting its shadows, seeking a glimpse of her, when a cloud shut the face of the moon and he could see nothing.

In the sudden darkness the figure on the lawn crouched. Fear stiffened Tessa's limbs but she took a step back, trying to wrap herself in deeper shadow. It was a mistake. She stumbled, and the sound brought the figure a crouching step nearer, stalking her. And worse. At that moment the moon found the edge of a cloud, dissolved its thin fringe and shone out.

Chuck was not looking at the full face of the moon, but he saw it. Its silver disc lay on the lawn, reflected in the pond, and he gazed directly at it, deliberately. Its bright glint shone in his eye, and a moment later the familiar dizziness had his fingers tightening on the sheet. The faintness passed and for a moment he thought nothing had happened except that he was standing on a wooden deck. And then he saw where he was. The deck was the window ledge, and he stood alongside his own gigantic hand. He looked up and saw the huge figure of himself gazing blankly into the moonlight and wondered briefly if he was breathing up there, but he turned away quickly because there were more important things to do.

A few paces away along the deck he saw what he was seeking. The nail he had hammered into the ledge was now as large as a bollard securing a ship to a quayside, but the cable that passed round it was the fishing line that curved steeply away to be lost in the darkness. He checked the paper clip. It was in position, looped round the line, and the pins lay gleaming beside it. He stooped to one of them, afraid it might be too large and heavy for what he had in mind, and he was relieved when he was able to close his hand around the shaft and pick it up with ease. It was true that the pinhead was cumbersome but, when he had slid the pin through his belt, the head rested comfortably at his waist like the hilt of a sword. He put the other sword at his other side. Then he stooped to the iron rods of the paper clip.

He manhandled it to the edge. There was a long drop below and the next part was going to be tricky. At least he had made sure that the clip was already hooked over the line, for he felt sure that if he had waited to do it when he was his present size it would have been too difficult, but he still had a problem. Once he had launched the clip over the edge he would not have the strength to prevent it sliding away while he settled himself safely inside its lower curve. He did not even have anything to tie himself in place.

He knew he was taking a risk, and he gave himself no time to think what might happen. He stepped quickly into the curve of the clip as it lay on the ledge, hoisted it up until the rods, almost as thick as his arms, were beneath both armpits and then, pushing it forward like a wheelbarrow, he stepped into space.

He fell through the night. The clip had become weightless, falling with him, and above him there seemed to be no line to take the strain. It must have broken. The rush of air blinded him. He was curled in a ball, clinging to the useless rods of the clip and ready for the sickening thud as he met the ground, when the air swirled in a new direction and he was slung sideways in a wide arc.

The pressure on his arms was too great and the rods were sliding from his grasp when the sideways swing eased and he glanced up to see the top of the clip hissing over the smooth filament. His elbows, crooked around the clip, held him as he plunged in a long, breathless fall that gradually flattened until the apple tree's huge leaves flicked by, at first only overhead, but then also underneath and on both sides so that he was in an airy cave with many bottomless passageways.

The metal loop above him slowed and then ceased its slide and he was swung forward to where a twig held out two great downward-curving leaves. His momentum carried him over them, but his backward swing caught him on the stem of a leaf and he clung to it, face down, riding it until the spring of the branch ceased trying to buck him off.

He clung until his breathing steadied, and then he began to ease himself from the loop. Each movement made the twig dip, but the leaves acted as sails to damp the swing, and he climbed to a thicker branch that lay horizontally overhead. He sat on it, legs astride, and hitched himself forward until the twig became broad enough to allow him to crawl and then, as the branches joined and became a roadway, he stood and walked.

He was on a solid, dark highway, and he was safe if he kept to the centre and did not wander to the edges where its roundness fell steeply away.

The branches made a city of aerial roads, some disappearing into leafy layers and only reappearing much further away, either thickening as they led inwards towards the trunk or becoming more slender and distant, balanced like thin bridges over giddy chasms. There were places where the leaves made tents or curved into layered domes big enough for houses, and he was the only walker in the whole of the shadowed city.

He had reached a fork where two broad roads joined, and had paused to get his bearings when a sound reached him from the well of darkness below. Some large creature stirred. It was stealthy, but he heard its weight shift and the sound of the breath in its nostrils.

'Tessa!' He sent his whisper down to the shades far below. 'Tessa!' Now he could see her hair spread on her shoulders.

He called her name again, louder, but she heard nothing. She was pressing back behind the trunk as the shape on the lawn stood upright and shed its skin.

17

Swordsmen

The shape shed its skin and a man stepped clear. Tessa saw the smooth cap of Peregrine Falconer's white hair and the cloak that had slid from his shoulders and lay crumpled at his feet. He had heard something and he advanced on the tree like a stalking animal.

She shrank back, panting, and was still attempting to hide when he reached the outermost branches and stooped to peer beneath the canopy of leaves.

Chuck, standing in the terraces of the branches, was a spectator in the roof of a dark theatre where great shadows moved. He saw Tessa, only half hidden by the trunk, and willed her not to move as the man's voice shifted the grains of darkness.

'Who's there?'

The voice buzzed like a night insect, and Peregrine Falconer's white head dipped under the outside fringe of the leaves as he came into the tree's shade.

'Is it you, boy?'

Tessa, her hands pressed against the trunk, stood still. The man, straightening, came another step forward, and now she was certain to be discovered.

'Run!' Chuck's yell was no more than the creak of a small branch among the dappled shadows as the moon struck down through the leaves.

'Tessa!'

Like the faintest of echoes in her brain, she heard her own name, but it was too late. The man stooped to come closer and in doing so he revealed the silver glint of the moon on water behind him. In that instant she helplessly fainted out of herself, and a moment later was clambering, waist-deep in moss, among the roots of the tree.

Chuck had found the loose line looped over the nail where he had left it. He let it drop, watching the loops uncoil until it hung straight down in the darkness. He grasped it and slid into the emptiness below.

The man moved cautiously, unable to see clearly in the depths of darkness under the tree. The line was invisible to him, and when it touched his face he brushed it away like a spider's web.

Chuck was still above him when the line jerked. His legs and arms clung tightly but it was useless. The line plucked itself away from him like a whiplash and he was spreadeagled in air. His fall was brief. Face down, he thudded into something solid and began to slide. He clawed at the surface with his fingers and they held.

He felt movement underneath him and slowly raised his head. He was on a mound covered in cloth and his fingers were clutching the coarse weave. He was confused for only a moment. Smallness was natural to him now and he saw he was on Peregrine Falconer's shoulder, clinging to his jacket. He crawled to the furrow made by the seam.

'Is that you, boy? Are you hiding there?'

The voice, coming from a head larger than the picture on a cinema screen, filled the air and put a vibration beneath Chuck as he inched his way along the furrow. And when the voice became silent, the breathing rose and fell like the sound of the sea surging in a cave. The shoulder heaved beneath him, but he rode it like an elephant and reached the collar where he steadied himself and gazed up into the waterfall of white hair. It swayed as Peregrine Falconer took another step, and the voice came again.

'Come out, young Master Hoskins, you have nothing to fear!'

Chuck looked ahead to where he knew Tessa was hidden. At this distance and in the lack of light the man could not be sure there was anybody there, but in two more paces he would be able to make out her shape as she pressed herself against the trunk.

Chuck had to act. He released both hands from the collar and reached up to the white hair. He grabbed it with both fists and, swinging his feet upwards to gain leverage, heaved back.

He heard a snort, the head jerked and he was flung sideways as the hair was torn from his grip and he was once more rolling along the shoulder, slipping and sliding on his back. One of the pin swords saved him. It caught in the material and dug deep. Too deep. He heard another exclamation, and a great hand came up to swat the stinging insect.

He could not escape. It was either fall or be crushed. He wrenched his sword free just as the hand came at him and all he could do was lunge directly at it. He felt the blade enter but it did not save him. The finger knocked him flat and then he was plunging down the front of the jacket. He hit the edge of a pocket and turned over. A button caught him a glancing blow and threw him outwards.

Tessa, cowering among the roots, heard the man's exclamation and saw his hand sweep something from his jacket. She caught a glimpse of a tiny shape cartwheeling in space, a glint of steel like a firefly's glow, heard the creak of grass stems bent suddenly double, a slither, then silence.

She forced her way through the dark forest of stems while, above her, the commotion ceased and the man stood still, straining his eyes to penetrate the darkness.

She saw Chuck. He was deep in a thicket of stems and using one of his swords to help himself to his feet.

'Chuck!' Her voice made him swing round, his sword ready to thrust, and she had to say his name again before he saw who it was and lowered the blade.

'I hadn't expected to see you my size,' he said.

'I couldn't help it. I saw the water flash.' She was still worried about his fall. 'Are you hurt?'

'I don't know yet.' He reversed his sword and handed it

to her. 'But you'd better have this,' he said. 'It's yours and it very nearly killed me.'

She took it, hardly hearing what he said. Danger still threatened. Somewhere in the darkness her large self was motionless, and already the man was moving again. A great foot swept through the shadows and crushed the grass near them.

Chuck said, 'We've got to stop him before he finds you.'

'We can't!'

'We can if we sting him!' he shouted. 'Sting him hard!'

The crushed grass helped them. They ran over its flattened stems, found the edge of his shoe and were clambering over the crossed hawsers of its laces just as it lifted to take another step. They edged upwards and towards his ankle and, in the momentary pause before the foot lifted again, they released their grip and stood upright.

'Ready?'

In the darkness he saw her nod.

'Now!'

They lunged, piercing deep, once, twice, three times before the battering hand came at them.

'Jump!'

They launched themselves from the swinging foot into the darkness.

18

The Storm

Peregrine Falconer stamped to rid himself of the wasps he believed were still stinging him, but Tessa and Chuck were clear of the pounding feet. They clung together as the ground shook beneath them, waiting until the tremors eased as the man retreated, running away from the swarm he was convinced he had disturbed.

Chuck raised his sword and shook it at the giant's back. 'The bigger they are,' he shouted, 'the harder they fall!'

Tessa was laughing with him. 'And the smaller they are the softer they come down.'

'Speak for yourself.' The edge of a blade of grass had rasped his arm as he leapt in the dark, but Tessa had been luckier. She had plunged into a tufted flower. 'Trust you to land in clover,' he said.

'Very funny.' She pointed her sword blade at the trunk of the tree where her other self was waiting, motionless. 'But what if he'd seen me there? Suppose he'd moved me somehow and I couldn't get back to myself.' She shuddered. The night suddenly seemed cold.

'It's even worse for me.' Chuck was thinking aloud. 'I left myself in my bedroom.'

'Trust you to say something like that.' She jabbed the ground angrily with her sword. 'You're thinking of nobody but yourself, Chuck Hoskins.'

'I'm not!'

'Oh yes you are. Even when I'm back inside myself I'm a long way from home—and you're tucked up in your little bed. You're a mummy's boy, that's what you are!'

'Oh am I? I only jumped on his shoulder just now and

swung on his hair. I just did it so that he wouldn't see you, that's all. That ain't much.'

'Well . . .' She was about to say more, but prevented herself. Her anger fell away. 'I didn't know you'd done that, Chuck.'

He shrugged. 'Well, some of it was an accident. I couldn't do anything else.'

She raised her eyes. 'You're being typical again.'

'What do you mean?'

'You've just done something most people would be proud of, but you won't admit it. You were brave, Chuck.'

'That makes two of us.'

They were facing each other in a glade among the grass stems and there was just enough light for him to see she was smiling. 'We're pretty good,' she said, 'considering we're so small.'

They were laughing now and they raised their swords to salute each other, making the blades clash, and then, without having to say a word, they wended their way through the forest of stems to where, beyond the tree, the grass was cut short and was no more than shoulder height.

Peregrine Falconer had picked up his cloak as he retreated and had reached the far side of the pool. He made a movement as though to put it over his shoulders but paused half way and turned to gaze out over the valley. His white hair was silvered for a moment in the moonlight and then the clouds, racing like horses in the sky, drew darkness with them and he changed his mind. Even though the cloak seemed very light, judging by the ease with which he swung it, it was bulky and made of some substance that rustled as he hung it over his arm.

They were straining their eyes in the dimness when something hissed through the air and made them cower. Whatever it was, it silenced itself in the grass, and they were raising themselves when it came again, closer this time, slicing down from the sky to burst close to Tessa. Spray chilled her arms.

'Rain!' she cried. Great globes of water, glinting like gigantic flasks, were swishing out of the sky and shattering all around them. 'Get under cover—we'll be drowned!'

Chuck did not move. Something else held his attention. The door of the house opened and shot a band of light across the lawn. Peregrine Falconer must have seen it because he moved swiftly to one side and was crouching, difficult to see, when a man's voice came from the doorway.

'It must be your imagination—there's nothing out there.'

For several seconds the man stood looking out, and then he stepped back and the door closed, nipping out the light. A moment later and he would have seen everything, for a flash of lightning put blue daylight into the garden and showed Peregrine Falconer huddled there. And with it, even before the thunder cracked in the clouds and rumbled down the valley like an avalanche, came a deluge.

Tessa was under the overhang of leaves but Chuck had gone forward, out in the open, and was already drenched by the ricochet of water splashes when the great glinting sphere of a raindrop battered him to the ground and exploded over him in a roaring cataract. He got to his feet and ran, head down, through the shrapnel of bursting drops and the lash of flailing grass to where Tessa was still protected.

'Look.' She pointed across the lawn. 'He's going.' Peregrine Falconer, holding his collar close to his neck, was squelching towards the far edge. 'Why doesn't he wear his cloak?' He seemed to be protecting it under his jacket. Lightning came again, and they saw that his hair was already plastered flat, and the next moment he slipped on the wet grass at the edge of the lawn and slithered quickly out of sight.

'He won't be able to stop till he gets to the bottom,' she said happily.

'It's all right for you to laugh. Just look at me.'

She did, and could not prevent herself from smiling. His clothes clung to him. 'Poor old Chuck,' she said, and had to step back because already the rainwater trickling through the grass had become a stream and was suddenly up to her ankles. They ran ahead of it to where the ground was still dry and climbed on to a tree root.

'I can't get back to my room while it's raining like this.' Chuck was shivering. 'I'd never make it.' He doubted if he could even climb the line back to the branch, and the long haul across to his window would be too much. His fingers were already so numb that his sword was slipping from them. 'I suppose that's another thing about being this size,' he said.

'What's that?' Tessa could hardly hear him above the roar of the rain, and his voice was weak. 'What did you say?'

'This size.' He had to clench his jaw to prevent his teeth chattering. 'When you're little you must get cold quicker. I'm so frozen I can hardly move.' He sat down and hugged his knees.

'Chuck.' She shook his shoulder. 'Stand up!'

'I don't want to.'

'Up!' She hauled him upright. 'Now stamp your feet! Wave your arms!' He seemed sleepy but she forced him to keep moving, fighting at the same time to keep the jerky panic out of her own breathing. He would never last like this. 'March!' she cried. 'Keep marching!'

They came down from the root on to a patch of bare earth and, once she saw that he would keep going, she ran ahead.

She found her own large shoe and climbed on to it. Standing on the toecap she tilted her head to look up. Shadows the size of buildings hung high overhead, overlapping and darkening, and somewhere up there her own face gazed without seeing.

'Hello!' She yelled at the top of her voice, but it was a tiny sound against the roar of the rain in the leaves. And nothing stirred. She found the lace holes of her shoe and steadied herself. She had to try again, but for a moment she was dumb. She must be mad to believe she was two people. It would prove that she was mad if she called out to herself as though she could not hear. And then the sudden terror of being divided, cut off from herself, made her shriek her own name.

'Tessa!'

Her own voice was a lost squeak in the darkness. She would have to climb, but the cuffs of her jeans were turned up, out of reach. And she had dressed so hurriedly she wore no socks. Her ankle was bare and smooth. Her only hope was the trunk of the tree and the long haul up to her hand. She turned, but stumbled on the tongue of her shoe and fell. She touched the skin of her ankle but slipped and, as she did so, she cried out.

The touch and the cry were the final grains needed to tilt a huge balance. Great shapes began to shift. They loomed over her, coming down. A huge hand and arm, and beyond them a face of enormous shadows. She felt no touch, but the whole night seemed to turn itself over, lifting her with it, and now she was no longer gazing up at great shapes but was herself a vast figure stooping down from the sky. She believed she was coming out of a dream, and expected to wake up in bed but found herself standing under a tree with rain cooling the air and beginning to drip through the leaves. She was her full size, out of doors on a wet night.

She searched and found him. Chuck saw her hand alongside him where he was still feebly marching, and he stepped across and lay down in her palm.

She cupped the tiny figure, and as the darkness closed around him he felt her warmth. He lay shivering, letting it seep into him.

'Chuck.' Her voice came gently to him through her fingers. 'You're not moving. Are you all right?'

He stood up, unsteady in the softness of her hand, and said, 'Can you hear me?'

'Yes,' she replied to the infinitely small sound trapped in her palm.

'Can you take me and put me down indoors?'

'But you're not strong enough, Chuck. And you're still drenched.'

He put his hand on his T-shirt. 'I'm almost dry.'

'You can't be!'

'I am, Tessa.' And suddenly the reason came to him. 'It's because I'm so small. My clothes must be like tissue, and you're hot-blooded, that's why.'

'I don't feel it. It's getting cold out here.' She opened her hand and saw him with his face tilted up towards her. 'You seem to be yourself again,' she said to the manikin. 'You're a sweet little thing, standing there.'

For what seemed a long time he said nothing. The only sound was the patter and rush of the rain and the distant growl as the next valley swallowed the thunder.

Then she was whispering to him. 'Hadn't I better let them know indoors? Shouldn't we tell them about us?' It was the only way he would be safe.

'No!' She could almost feel his sharp cry against her skin.

'Why not? You wanted everybody to know yesterday.'

'But that's not now.' Everything had changed. She had just saved his life, and nobody else had helped. He did not want anybody to know. 'It's nothing to do with them,' he said. 'They'd spoil it. It's a secret!'

She knew it was. There was too much now to pass on. But she was very afraid for him.

'It will be dangerous, Chuck.'

'I've got it all worked out. All you've got to do is get me into the house.'

There was a pause in which she gazed down at him without answering.

'Please, Tessa. Don't spoil everything.'

She cupped her other hand over him to protect him from the rain and moved out from the shelter of the tree.

19

Black Blood

Chuck had told her the door would not be locked, but what if it was? Her hair was clinging to her cheeks as she climbed the steps from the lawn, but at least the swish of the rain on the flagstones blotted out all other sound and she moved silently nearer the house.

There was a chink of brightness between the curtains in the room to her right, and a dim light from the hall showed through panels of coloured glass alongside the door. She held him so that he could see.

'All clear.' His whisper was less than the hiss of the rain and she had to strain to make out his words. 'The hall's empty.'

She closed her fingers gently over his head, and with her other hand reached for the door handle. It turned easily, there was a faint squeak from the hinges as the door swung inwards just enough for her to get her arm through the gap.

'Good luck.' She mouthed the words without sound but she saw him wave and raise his sword to her and then, as she stooped, he slid down the slope of her fingers and was gone.

She pulled the door closed. The click of the lock startled her, but it was only one extra sound in the gurgle of the rain in the gutters and nobody raised the alarm as she vanished through the gate into the lane.

In the hall the amber light was part of the silence. The chairs and the hall table slumbered in it, and the tiles at the edge of the rug gleamed softly like deserted streets. The gleam followed him as he crossed the squares and climbed on to the carpet at the foot of the stairs. Under the overhang of the bottom stair he lost sight of the slope mounting above him and wished he had strung an emergency line from the landing as he had once thought of doing but had abandoned for fear of it being discovered. He had, however, examined the route and there was an alternative.

Although the red stair carpet rose sheer above him, it was grooved with a pattern that made wriggling channels into which he could almost squeeze his body. And there was something else that helped him. The surface of the carpet was fluffy, but within the grooves it was woven in loops which, when he tested them with his hands and feet, made a ladder of hard, twisted cords. He put his sword through his belt and began to climb.

The overhang from step to step was not great and he made good progress, resting each time he hauled himself over the edge of a tread. It was lonely work, scaling cliff after cliff in the night, and when he had two to go he lay back on the fluffy pile of the carpet and rested. He thought of Tessa and wondered if she had been able to get back into her own house without being discovered and what she would do to prevent her mother finding her wet clothes in the morning. He listened to the trickle and drip of the rain as it washed down pipes and into drains where there were mysteries that only the Tin Soldier had ever discovered. The house itself ticked and made noises, small pattering sounds that faded and repeated, advancing and receding like gentle breathing. He was listening to them, stretched out on the soft red bed of the carpet, when his eyes closed.

The spider's six eyes could not be closed. They missed nothing as it skirmished along the landing looking for prey. It had had a bad night's hunting, and the fat bag of its body slung inside its cradle of legs was hungry.

It reached the edge of the top step and halted. Two of the six eyes picked out objects below. The next stair was vacant, but on the lip of the next a meal waited to be immobilized by its poison fangs. Its front legs reached over the edge, and then the head studded with eyes and the plump sack of its body tilted and began the descent.

A burst of noise startled Chuck awake. There was more light. He rolled over. Beyond the banisters the great void of the hall was filled with voices. He crawled to the edge and looked down. His mother had come from the bright light of the open door to stand in the hall and was talking to someone still inside the room.

'Try to be quiet,' she said. 'He's asleep—or should be.' She raised her head to look up and gazed straight at Chuck without seeing him. 'I don't want him to know just yet.'

'Does he suspect?' It was the man's voice that Chuck had heard in the garden.

'I don't know. You can never tell. But he was so upset when I told him I wanted to sell this house that I thought . . . I really thought I'd done something terrible to him.' The man chuckled but she quietened him. 'Listen to me. He began acting strangely. Said the most peculiar things. I think,' she paused, 'I think that girl had something to do with it. I think they are encouraging each other. They've got secrets; far too many of them.'

This time the man's chuckle was louder. He was half way through the door, but the shadows of the hall meant that all Chuck could see of him was the top of his dark head. 'If she's the kid I'm thinking of, I don't blame him for anything.'

'No,' she protested, 'don't be like that. It's unhealthy at their age.'

'But not at ours?'

The spider had made its vertical descent and came scuttling to the edge of the stair tread above Chuck. He had heard the faint scratch of its claws but only at the back of his mind. His attention was concentrated below. The man was speaking.

'Trudy, they're nice kids. Leave them alone.'

'But there are other things. He's beginning to speak so badly. I do think he ought to go away to school, really I do, before it's too late.'

'Too late for what?' The man stood directly under the hall light. And now, in spite of the long shadows that streaked his face, Chuck knew who he was. 'I hope you don't mean it's too late for this,' said Bob Wood, putting his arms around Chuck's mother.

Chuck turned away. He scanned the stairs but saw nothing—not even the six eyes above him. A murmur from below made him turn again. His mother had lifted her face to Bob Wood and they were kissing.

Chuck jerked his head around just as the spider moved. Now, for the first time, he saw the specks of white light gleam in the six eyes, and the eight legs fingering their way downwards. He saw it all and felt no fear. Too much was happening for fear. He hauled the pin-sword from his belt and went to meet the angling legs and the mouth with the many moving parts.

The spider stopped, allowing him to come nearer. He saw its mouth palps sieving the air, and its two poison fangs spread wide, but nothing could stop him. He went closer until the spider, reaching out with one hairy leg, touched his shoulder, fingering its food.

It was then that he lunged with his sword, stabbing. He felt the point bite and the leg jerked back. Very delicately, the claw touched the ground, and the bag body sank within the lobster pot of the spider's legs as it prepared to launch itself.

Somewhere there were soft voices. He heard them like a lullaby in the back of his mind as he went into battle. He ran into the mesh of legs, drew back his arm and with all his force plunged his sword into the gape of the fangs. The point stuttered against something hard and the shock rolled him over. In the same instant the spider's legs contracted and gripped him in a rasp of stiff hairs.

Only his arm was free and he heaved the blade up and back and stabbed again, and then again and he kept stabbing until his hand was covered in blue-black blood and the legs quivered and fell away.

20
Bob Wood

You don't normally break into people's houses to find out what they're up to, which is what Tessa and me should have done to Peregrine Falconer next morning. That came later, and we were practically forced into it. What we did to start with was have an argument.

We were down by the stream, leaning against the railings of the bridge, when Tessa said, 'Why are you looking at me like that?'

I didn't know she'd seen me. 'I was thinking,' I said.

'What about?' She *never* lets you off the hook.

'*Gulliver's Travels*,' I said.

'Mm.' She nodded like mad. 'I sometimes think about that as well. About all the little people in Lilliput—just like us. It makes you think you've got inside a story somehow—it ain't everybody who can do that.'

'I didn't mean Lilliput,' I said. 'I meant the place where he was normal size but all the other people were giants and they could pick him up like a button.'

'Same thing.'

'No it's not.'

'Well anyway,' she said, 'I'm glad last night's over. It's lovely to be warm again.'

The stream was still running deep after the storm in the night but the sun was shining, and I should have just agreed with her and left it at that, but I've also got the sort of mind that won't let go. Sometimes. 'Gulliver got it wrong about the giants,' I said.

'You ain't still on about that, are you?' she said, and then she came out with what was really on her mind. 'Was Bob

Wood really kissing your mum? I mean, did she let him?'

I said, 'The queen of the giants seemed to be beautiful until she picked Gulliver up and then he saw the pores of her skin and everything and he thought she was ugly.'

That had Tessa looking up at the sky. 'Well I suppose she was ugly. Everybody is if you look close enough.'

'Not you,' I said. That's what had been on my mind all morning, but now I'd said it I felt embarrassed. Sometimes you can say too much.

'Oh,' she said. She looked surprised. 'I'd forgotten you'd seen me like that.'

'I thought I'd see only a part of you at a time, like Gulliver, when you picked me up. But I didn't, I saw you all at once.'

'But big,' she said. 'Huge.'

Then I told her something I often think. 'Things sometimes seem very big and very small at the same time,' I said. 'When I was a little kid and went into a cathedral I never dared push against those columns that hold up the roof because I knew I could push them over if my mind said so. I knew I could.' I only told her about it because it seemed to be what we were doing, both of us. 'You could have breathed me in, but you were still like yourself,' I said. 'Not ugly.'

I was chicken. What I wanted to say was that she was even prettier, but I didn't dare. But I think she knew because she turned her head away, and when her hair fell alongside her face and hid it she didn't brush it back like she normally did. She just stayed like that, looking up the hill towards the pub and the green. And the next thing that happened spoiled everything.

'Help!' she said, not very loud but she looked as if she wanted to run away—which I would have agreed with except it was too late because Bob Wood was already coming down the road towards us. We'd been so busy talking we hadn't seen him. It was me who started to run, but Tessa wouldn't let me. She dug her nails into my arm.

'Good morning, Mr Wood,' she said, but I didn't say anything. I didn't like him. He was trying to be friendly, but that only made it worse.

I saw Chuck's face and he'd gone ugly. His eyes were hard and his whole face had just pinched up so all you could see was how much he hated Bob Wood. And it wasn't fair. It wasn't Bob Wood's fault he liked Trudy Hoskins. It wasn't her fault either—I even began to like Chuck's mum just because Bob Wood did. I was in a tangle.

But the worst thing was when he put his hand on the railing next to Chuck's, and Chuck moved away. It wasn't much, but Bob Wood's smile suddenly went away and where the wrinkles had been at the corners of his eyes there were little pale streaks where the sun hadn't reached. He even looked as if Chuck scared him. It was terrible to see a man afraid of a boy.

'I was up at your place last night, Chuck,' he said, and you could tell his mouth was dry.

'I know,' said Chuck.

'I thought so.' Bob Wood was trying to smile as he said it. 'I hope you didn't get too wet out there on the grass.'

Chuck's head jerked towards him and he said, 'That wasn't me!' And Bob Wood just looked past him and smiled at me and said, 'Well somebody was.'

He thought it was me but he couldn't have seen me, and he couldn't have seen Chuck either. What he saw must have been Peregrine Falconer, but I knew Chuck didn't want anybody to know about that any more so I let him think he must have seen us having a midnight picnic, and I said, 'We sheltered until it was all over.'

He gave his head a shake as if he didn't want to know all our secrets, and that would have been all right except that Chuck wouldn't leave it alone. Before I could do anything to stop him he glared at Bob Wood and said straight out, 'And I saw you last night, and I know why Trudy wants to send me away to school. She says it's because of the way I speak, but that ain't nothing to do with it. She's got another reason, ain't she?'

'Now hold on a minute, mate.' Bob Wood sounded just as if he was talking to a man. 'Aren't you jumping to conclusions?'

There was no stopping Chuck now. 'She'd never sell our house if she knew everything I do,' he said. 'She'd never let that man Falconer have it, because he can rule everybody if he gets it. He can, because that pond is the falcon's eye and it can make people go small, and once he knows how to do it he'll be in charge of the whole valley just like they used to be!'

He gave it all away. Everything. And he was the one who said it should be secret. The only good thing was that Bob Wood didn't know what to make of it, so I grabbed Chuck's arm and I said, 'Come on, Mr Wood doesn't want to hear all that.'

I knew Chuck was going to say something else, but it was even worse than I expected. He suddenly pointed up the slope and we saw his mother was walking across the green. 'There she is,' he said to Bob Wood. 'I expect she wants to kiss you again.'

He spun round then, and I had to run to catch him up. He didn't once look back. But I did. I saw Chuck's mother and Bob Wood standing side by side, and all of a sudden I wanted to wave to them but then I remembered what she thought of me so I ducked my head down and didn't lift it until after we got round a bend in the road.

What I didn't know was that we were caught in a whirlpool. At that moment we were right on the fringes of it and it was going to sweep us down the valley and put us in a lot of danger, but I didn't feel it because it began in such a gentle sort of way.

'Oh, I wish,' I said, and then I didn't want to say anything else.

'Wish what?' he said.

'Nothing.' I hadn't meant the words to come out. I just

wished his mother liked me a bit more, and I wished he hadn't been so horrible to Bob Wood. I wished a lot of things and I needn't have said anything about them, but I did. We were walking in a sunken road between the banks of two fields, and I must have felt protected because I didn't feel the whirlpool rushing when I said to him, 'You didn't look back once. You didn't see them.'

'I didn't want to.'

Then the whirlpool tugged at me. 'I heard my mum say something about Bob Wood once. Do you want to hear?'

'No.'

'He used to live here when he was a boy. That's why everybody knows him.'

'Except me.'

'And you don't count,' I said. 'But my mum knows him ever so well, and so does Dad. And anyway he doesn't live far away now—just over the hill in Stokeley. He hires out tractors and combines.'

'So what?'

'So nothing,' but I couldn't stop now. 'I heard my mum tell my dad once she could never understand why Bob Wood never got married because lots of girls was after him, and not just because of his money. Anyway he didn't have none then, not like now. It was because he was so quiet and nice lookin'.'

Chuck stared at me then so that I almost curled up, but I wasn't going to have him bully me, so I said, 'Well he *is* nice lookin', even if he is going a bit grey. And there's somethin' else you don't know because you was so full of yourself you didn't take the trouble to turn your head. I saw your mum and him standing together just now and you could tell something about them. You could tell.'

'You're crying,' he said. He was really nasty.

'I don't care. They like each other. Anybody can tell that.'

'I saw them,' he said. 'Last night.'

'No you didn't. You don't see anything. All you see is yourself.'

'You'd better wipe your eyes,' he said, and I did, with my fingers, but words were rushing out as I did it.

'You never even saw that man just now, did you? He was lookin' at you as if he was afraid of you.'

Chuck just shrugged, but I could see I'd made him think about what he'd just done, and I suppose I should have been sorry for him, but I wasn't. I said, 'I ain't never going to forget the way Bob Wood looked at you. All he wanted to do was be friendly, and what did you do? You turned your back on him!'

Chuck didn't look at me. He said, 'Well he shouldn't have been in my house last night.'

'Oh you!' I could hardly think of any words. 'Oh you,' I said, 'do you think you're the only person in the world whose father's dead!'

The whirlwind caught hold of me then and swirled me away. I just ran. I didn't care where I was going.

21

The Painted Bird

She kept ahead of him as they ran away from the village. The woods were thick on this side of the valley, and the road climbed steeply until it reached the trees. When it levelled out she called over her shoulder, 'Race you, mummy's boy!' and plunged into the endless greenhouse of the trees.

Few cars passed this way and a line of weeds grew along the centre of the road. The overgrown verges were still wet from the night's rain, but the sun was penetrating the roof of leaves and the heat was green and ferny. She was out of breath and the footsteps at her back were gaining on her when the tall gateposts came in sight at the roadside, and in one desperate lunge she got there first and clung to the gate, her lungs heaving.

'Beat you!' It was a gasp.

'I wasn't racing.'

'Yes you were. Ask anybody.'

He also held the iron bars. 'Ain't anybody here to ask. Anyway you chet.'

'Chet?'

'Cheated. That's what you done.'

'Did.'

'That's right—you did. You chet.'

She swung back on the bars, laughing. 'You'll have to learn to speak better than that at your new school, Charles Hoskins.'

'Theresa Barton had better shut up.'

'Now you're being uncouth, Charles.'

'I've warned you . . .' He moved towards her but she

released her grip on the bars and stood back.

'You know where we are, Chuck, don't you?' Her voice had dropped. The driveway beyond the gate curved towards Creance Hall, where old Mrs Falconer had died. Peregrine Falconer lived there now. 'He might be able to see us.'

'I doubt it,' said Chuck. 'It looks deserted.'

Shrubs had encroached on the driveway so that all they could see was part of the doorway between its pilasters and some of the upper windows where linen blinds were pulled down like the thin eyelids of somebody dead.

'I don't like it,' she said. 'Let's go back.' But Chuck had already tried the gate handle and it turned. He pushed and the gate began to swing. There was not even a creak from rust. 'What are you doing!' She tried to pull him back. 'Close it, quick.'

He checked the swing of the gate. There would be no disgrace in pulling it shut and going away. Nobody could possibly blame him. The house belonged to someone else and he had no right to creep towards it like a thief.

'Come on, Chuck.'

She tugged at him and he made up his mind. His father had hated thieves and people who spied. He pulled at the gate, hauling it shut. It moved easily, but as he leant back he saw the stone figure of a falcon that crowned the gatepost. Only one. The other had gone. Crumbled away. Flown. And suddenly his father's map overruled everything. Falcon. The whole hawk valley. Some of its secrets lay here and if he pulled the gate closed he would shut it out for ever.

He leant on the bars just before the gate clicked shut. 'All right, Dad,' he murmured. 'I suppose I've got to.'

Tessa had not heard his words. 'What did you say?' she asked.

'I'm going to take a look.' He turned towards her, hoping she would plead with him, forcing him to turn back. 'Just to make sure,' he said.

Her eyes sought him out. She saw what was in his mind and her courage was more than his. She gave him no choice. 'I'm scared,' she said.

'That makes two of us.' He tried to grin as he pushed the gate wide enough for them both to enter, and she went with him and closed it softly behind them.

They kept close to the overhanging shrubs, walking on the moss that edged the gravel until the driveway opened into a wide semicircle and the full face of the house loomed at them across the space. They dipped into the bushes and worked their way to the right, keeping their eyes on the blank windows until they reached the corner. The side of the house was as blind as the front and stood guard over a silence that deepened second by second.

'That's far enough,' she whispered, but he had to obliterate his hesitation at the gate. He had to prove himself.

'I want to see what's at the back,' he said.

'It'll be just like the front.' She wanted to prevent him, but she saw from the corner of her eye that he meant to move forward, so she went first. They were matching each other, dare for dare.

They skirted the gravel but still had to cross open ground before they reached the shelter of a tall stone wall that stretched around the back of the house and disappeared among the dense trees of the hillside. There was an archway set in it wide enough to take a carriage, and as they edged closer they saw that it was open, without a gate. Through it they glimpsed a paved courtyard and a row of buildings.

'Stables,' Tessa whispered. 'It's an old stable yard.'

They crept further forward until they stood beneath the arch. The yard held the heat of the clear morning and a silence so intense it was as though they could hear the sun at its slow work of turning stone into dust.

To their right was a row of coach houses with their tall doors padlocked, but the side of the square directly

121

opposite them was taken up entirely by a single long building. It had two doors, widely spaced, and small slatted windows. Its plain face could have been that of a storeroom or an old workshop—except for one thing. At the centre of its frontage and stretching from the gutter of its low roof to the ground, a massive coat of arms had been cut into the stone. And it was coloured. With plainness everywhere else, its gaudiness drew Chuck forward.

'Just look at the size of it!' he said. 'Do you see what it is?'

'Of course I do. And keep your voice down!' She was alongside him, looking fearfully from left to right as she stepped carefully over the dried and brittle grass in the cracks between the flagstones. A single night's rain had done nothing to freshen it. 'It's the same as the shield in the church.'

It was like the side of the Falconer tomb, but this coat of arms was complete. The bird dominated its centre.

'Look at the size of it!' Chuck repeated. He started forward. 'That falcon must be as big as a man. Bigger than me, anyway.'

He went up to it and stood with the stone bird towering over him, its talons clutching the painted bridge.

It made her nervous to see him there, and she glanced towards the house. One row of windows overlooking the yard was unshuttered.

'Chuck!' Her urgent whisper made him turn towards her, and she pointed. 'That's where he must live. He could see us!'

They stood motionless, watching. The glass of the windows caught the cloudless sky and gazed back at them. If there was any movement behind the blue glare it was far back, hidden.

'All right,' he said, 'we'll go,' but he lingered to prove he was not being driven away by fear. 'I'd still like to know why that coat of arms is so huge.'

They backed away keeping their eyes on it, fascinated by

its size. It was out of place—the only decoration in the entire yard, squatting under the low roof like an animal that had outgrown its cage.

'Why?' he said. 'Why is a building like that so important?'

He was speaking to himself, but he had been overheard. A voice behind their backs answered him.

'That bird speaks for itself, I think.'

22

Hanging Falcon

The voice jolted them, and their hands came together and gripped.

'It speaks for itself, I think.'

They jerked around.

'If you look, and if you listen, it speaks.'

In the sunlight of the square, between them and the archway, the slight grey figure with its crest of white hair was poised as though, like the seed of a dandelion, it had at that moment drifted down.

'I have been listening,' said Peregrine Falconer. 'I can hear the twitch of a mouse and the footfall of a beetle. I can hear the sun beating on a wall. I have been listening for you since the outer gate clicked shut.'

It was impossible that he could have heard it. Tessa opened her mouth, but a large hand was raised to silence her.

'My dear young lady, I know the gate is at some distance and that you were at pains to close it quietly—but this whole domain is a place of infinite silence, like one great listening ear, so that the flutter of a moth vibrates with the pulse of a beating drum.' He paused, and a smile seeped into the wrinkles of his long face. 'Beating as loudly as certain hearts are pounding at this moment, I do not doubt.'

'Not mine.' From a dry mouth, Chuck struggled to speak. 'We haven't done anything.'

The little man waited until, easing their fingers free, they turned fully around to face him, and then he spoke to Tessa.

'This boy,' he said, 'is as brave as a lion. And, as I have had occasion to remark to another person known to him, he has a pulsating intelligence. He is, in fact, a masterpiece among boys,' and then, bowing towards her, he added, 'as, I do not doubt, you are a gem among young ladies.'

'We didn't mean any harm,' she said.

'Naturally not!' He had raised his voice so that its edge sawed at the air, and he moved a step nearer. 'But tell me, does anybody know where you are?'

'Yes,' lied Chuck, and Tessa said quickly, 'I told my mother.'

'Indeed? And why, pray, have you made this excursion?' His twinkling smile had a cutting edge. 'Why have I the pleasure of your company?'

'I was curious.' Chuck let his words tell the truth. 'I wanted to know what it was like here.'

'We both did,' said Tessa.

'Excellent. Excellent.' The smile remained. 'So you let everybody know of your secretive little expedition to Creance Hall?'

He had seen through the lie. Chuck tried to moisten his mouth but it remained dry. Neither of them spoke.

'No matter.' A hand too large for a man of his short stature waved their offence to one side but hovered in front of his chest with its fingers bent like a crouching crab. It could scuttle and catch. 'I am charmed to have you here. Flattered by your interest. No—don't leave me.' They had moved, but the hand barred their way. 'You have had the courtesy to call on me, so you must not deny me the pleasure of making you welcome.'

Both hands made a graceful gesture, indicating that he wished them to turn around. They did so, slowly, but edging sideways so that he was not completely out of their sight.

'Let us advance.'

His manner of speaking was an irritation, spinning a web with a voice that was now silky but could not be disobeyed. Still with arms slightly outspread he shepherded them towards the building dominated by the coat of arms, and for the first time Tessa noticed the bars of the small windows set in the doors. It was too much like a prison-house. She twisted her head to ask where he was taking them but was met by the full force of his smile. His teeth showed slightly, and he nodded as though he knew what was in her mind. 'All will be clear in a moment, my dear,' he murmured. 'Your questions will be answered.'

They walked until the coat of arms loomed over them, and the huge bird, painted as black as a funeral monument, gazed above their heads with an eye made fierce by a touch of red. Its claws were carved crudely over the stone bridge.

The silence was broken by Peregrine Falconer's chuckle. 'The badge of the Falconers. An impressive fowl, don't you think? And do you see those talons—he holds the whole valley in his foot.'

Tessa found her voice. 'Only the bridge,' she said. 'That's Jessie's Bridge.'

'Indeed and indeed it is.' His smile showed more teeth. 'But Jessie's Bridge—why Jessie's Bridge—how did it come by the name do you think?'

It was better to speak than stay silent. 'It must have been somebody called Jessie,' she said.

His face was like a wrinkled glove inside which fingers were flexing. His smile was snatched away but came again, and suddenly, with such speed that she gave a little shriek, he snatched Tessa by the wrist and tugged her forward. No sooner had his hard fingers grasped her than she was released and he was pointing at the carved stonework, at ribbons that fluttered from the legs of the falcon. 'And these, what are these?' He turned to face them, and when they gave no answer, he said, 'They are the thongs that the falconer holds when the bird is on his glove. They have a name. They are the jesses.' His eyes gleamed. 'The bridge of the jesses. Jessie's Bridge. How obvious!'

Tessa rubbed her wrist. He was no longer between them

126

and the entrance to the courtyard. They could run. He was making no effort to pen them in.

And now his voice was wheezing eagerly and his eye was on Chuck. 'And Creance Hall. Why Creance?'

He immediately answered his own question. 'Because the creance was the leash that tethered the falcon to his block. And if you seek for the hall, you shall find even that.' He pointed to where a house was cut crudely into the stonework, half obscured by the falcon's wing. 'Did I not tell you everything is here, if you can but read?'

Chuck drew in his breath. They were being led forward, treading on a shell that hid great mysteries, and he must not reveal how much he already knew. But there was one thing he had to find out.

'If the hawk has a thong around its legs,' he said, 'why does it need a golden chain around its neck?'

He had touched a dangerous point. The smile faltered, almost vanished, then came again. 'A chain of gold? A *golden* chain? I beg you to look closer.'

They tilted their heads to look at the carved head close to the eaves of the building. The chain that lay around the hawk's shoulders was made of square links, and they were certainly painted gold. But in the centre, resting on the bird's breast, were two larger, circular links, and only one of them was gilded. The other was silver.

'How very strange.' Peregrine Falconer appeared to be teasing them now. 'Gold and silver. Silver and gold. Yet there is no doubt about the chain and what that may mean. The chain is a sign of mastery and it binds the valley to the falcon and the ferocity of its Quelling Eye.' He had emphasized the words, but now he paused and spoke lightly. 'Or so the legend goes. No doubt you know of that.'

Tessa's courage was returning. 'I've heard of the Quelling Eye,' she said, 'but I don't understand it.'

'Kings and warriors have it, my child. It is the fierce glare that subdues their enemies.'

'Is that all?' She spoke with such innocence that Chuck's skin turned cold. She was about to test how much the man knew. 'I thought it meant something magic,' she said, 'like turning all your enemies very small.'

Peregrine Falconer was pleased with her. 'What a poetic imagination you have, my dear young lady. I have no doubt but that the victims of the Quelling Eye would shrink in their shoes and feel very small indeed.'

'I didn't mean that,' she said, and frightened Chuck into interrupting.

'What about the gold and silver?' he said. 'You were going to tell us about that.'

'Was I?' The long face frowned at him, displeased. 'The young lady's flight of fancy drove it from my mind. There is magic in her imagination, is there not?'

'I don't know.'

'You don't know!' He breathed in so sharply that his nostrils narrowed. 'There are more things in heaven and earth than are dreamt of in your philosophy, young Master Hoskins. Great wonders. Magical things!'

'I know.' Chuck's nervousness increased. The little man was turning against him.

'The eye that quells and the wings that fly. Where do you find them both combined?' He paused only to turn away from them and sweep his hand upwards towards the huge bird, lifting himself on his toes. For an instant he seemed to take on the bird's power, growing huge and glaring down on them. They stepped back, and when he saw the effect he had made he allowed his smile to return.

'Gold and silver,' he said. 'You are mystified by gold and silver, as many have been before you. Come with me.'

Abruptly he walked away along the wall of the low building until he came to a door. He stopped and beckoned, and when he saw that they were reluctant he beamed at them. 'Don't be afraid. This is no prison despite the bars. I shall not lock you away.'

They could easily have made a break for it, running

across the yard and out, but curiosity held them now. They went forward. Through the bars in the opening in the door they saw a whitewashed wall and partitions like the stalls in a stable but far too small for any horse. It was not to show them what lay inside the building that Peregrine Falconer had beckoned them forward; he was pointing at the lintel above the door. There was an inscription incised in the stonework with the letters picked out in paint. 'Gold and silver,' he said. 'The answer is there for all to see.'

Although the lettering was old-fashioned, the words were easy to read:

'When Gold and Silver Reign on High,
The Master of the Quelling Eye,
Shall like a Falcon mount the Sky.'

Chuck went through it a second time. 'I don't get it,' he said. 'It doesn't tell me anything.'

The wrinkled face had the kind of intelligence that looks out from a monkey's eyes, deep but wordless. It was turned towards Tessa, almost as though he expected her to give an explanation of the rhyme. She disappointed him.

'I don't understand it either,' she said.

'Then it is a riddle.' The voice wheezed and whispered around the square, and he turned away.

Behind his back, Chuck looked at Tessa and shrugged. His fear of Peregrine Falconer was dwindling.

'What does it mean?' Chuck asked.

'It is plain to those who see.' There was no smile on the man's face now.

'Aren't you going to tell us?'

'It will become plain before long.' Suddenly Peregrine Falconer's patience was wearing thin. 'Now I must ask you to leave.'

He took a step away from the door, expecting them to follow, but Chuck's daring was increasing. 'You haven't told us what this place is,' he said. 'Is it a stable?'

'For hawks,' said Peregrine Falconer. 'The Falconers *were* falconers and this is where they housed their birds of prey. It is the Falconer mews.'

Even before Chuck had worked it out, Tessa understood why the coat of arms was so huge. Hawks were the Falconers' pride. She took a step forward and looked through the bars. The partitions stretched the length of the building, and in front of each stall a block of wood sawn from the trunk of a tree stood on the brick floor. The wood was old and grey and scarred by the talons of many birds, but the long row was vacant and still, as it must have been for many years.

'Young lady, it is time to leave.'

She was turning to obey when she saw that there was, after all, something else in the mews. It was suspended from a rafter, just clear of the stalls and the wooden blocks. It was a large shape, bulky and lifeless, indistinct in the shadows. Below it was what appeared to be another shadow until she saw that a fluid had dripped from it and formed a dark pool on the brick floor.

'Young lady!'

The shape hung limply like the dripping skin of a flayed animal, and swung to a shift in the air. There was a footstep behind her and a touch on her arm that made her back away just as the skin turned slowly and she saw the creature's grey head dangling forward. The shape was a bird, with its dead head hanging slackly against its breast. It was a falcon as large as a man.

23

Silver and Gold

'It wasn't blood,' said Chuck. 'It couldn't have been.'

'Why not?'

'Because there isn't a bird that big, that's why. It wasn't an animal either, and it wasn't human. I know what it was, and so do you.'

'You didn't see it.' Her limbs were stiff, still clamped by fear even though she and Chuck had walked free from the Hall and now the trees were behind them and they were in the sun. 'It had feathers,' she said, 'and it was dripping.'

'Rain.' He turned so that he was walking backwards in front of her. 'It was his cloak drying out after he got caught in the thunderstorm.'

'It had a head. A huge head.'

'It's a helmet. A hawk helmet. I saw it last night.'

She looked at him as he retreated in front of her. His chunky face was battered and lopsided and would have seemed to be much older if it hadn't been for his eyes. They were wide and blue and she could read them. He was worried about her. 'You couldn't have seen anything,' she said. 'It was too dark.'

He didn't try to defend himself. 'He wears it because he thinks he's going to fly. It's a flying cloak. He's going to fly like a falcon and pick off his enemies like beetles.'

She felt the skin of her arms roughen and she hugged herself, shivering in spite of the sun. Chuck was right. The little man believed he could do it. 'He's mad,' she said. The thought of him prancing in the darkness, believing in magic, was even worse than if he really could fly. The ghastly dripping cloak was part of a madman's mind. 'He's all twisted up,' she said. 'I wish we'd never seen anything. I wish nothing had happened.'

His eyes rested on her a moment longer. He knew what she meant. If Peregrine Falconer was mad, so were they. He turned so that he was walking alongside her, soberly. 'And the Quelling Eye must only be a sort of hypnotism,' he said. 'That makes sense.'

It did make sense. And the day became drab. Last night she had picked him up in her hand and warmed him and saved his life. But it had all been pretence, something they had imagined.

'Have you got a diary?' she said.

They walked a few paces before the question sank in. 'What do you want a diary for?' he said. 'I can tell you the date if that's what you want to know.'

'Sometimes, Chuck Hoskins, I could bat you across the head with somethin'. As if I'd want a diary for that—I *know* the date.'

'That's more than I do, as a matter of fact. And if you bat me I'll bat you back.'

'Hit a girl, that's just about what you would do.'

They had crossed the bridge and reached the edge of the green. She slapped at him and he put his arms over his head and ran. She chased him around the seat where old people waited for buses, and when he allowed himself to be caught she pummelled him. Neither of them saw his mother come out of the Falconer's Arms with Bob Wood, and Chuck was lying on the seat, still covering his head, when Tessa heard a man's laugh and then his voice.

'Every time I come across these two they're in a scrap.'

She looked up. It wasn't Bob Wood she saw first, it was Chuck's mother, and she was looking far from pleased.

Tessa stood up and took a step backwards. I'm rough, she thought, and I look it. Why does she have to see me like this?

The injustice of it brought a prickle of tears to the corners of her eyes but she refused to brush them away.

Bob Wood made it worse. As Chuck's head came up, he said, 'The first time I saw these two, Trudy, they'd taken on a whole gang of roughs down by the stream there. Doing all right, too, they was.'

The village accent must have been for Tessa's benefit. She hated him for it and was on the verge of letting him know the way village people really spoke when they were angry when Chuck butted in.

'We would have been all right,' he said to Bob Wood, 'except we was outnumbered.'

'Were,' said his mother. '*Were* outnumbered.' She carefully did not let her eyes rest on Tessa.

'That's put you in your place,' said Bob Wood, and Chuck saw his mother smile sheepishly. 'What about it then, Chuck, still in trouble I see?'

'She was just asking if I'd got a diary,' he said.

'She must want to know the date pretty bad if she strikes you over the head to get it.'

Chuck could not stop himself laughing, but Tessa was exasperated.

'It's not the date!' she cried. 'What I want is a diary with one o' them . . . one of those little moons in so's you can tell when it's full moon. That's all.'

Bob Wood had his jacket hooked on one finger and slung over his shoulder. He swung it round and searched in an inside pocket. 'Here you are then, gal, take a look at that. There ain't no secrets in it.' He looked towards Trudy and cleared his throat. '*Aren't* no secrets,' he said, and this time it was Tessa who wanted to laugh. She took the little book quickly to disguise the way she felt and sat down.

She was leafing through it when Chuck sat down beside her and asked, 'What's so important, Tessa?'

'It's the chain.' She was whispering, not wanting anybody else to hear. 'Those two rings. Gold and silver . I've got an idea.' She turned the pages feverishly. 'What *is* the date, anyway?'

'June the twenty-first.'

133

She found it. 'Look.' Her finger rested on the little ring alongside the day in the diary. 'That's full moon. The silver ring. Tonight.' She had made herself learn the rhyme as she looked at it in the courtyard, and now she quoted the first line, 'When Gold and Silver reign on high.'

Chuck felt a shiver of something suddenly coming right, but it was not complete. 'There's still the gold ring,' he said. 'What's that?' But he knew even before she told him.

'It's the sun,' she said. 'It's got to be.'

Chuck's head was close to hers. 'And linked,' he said. 'They've got to come together somehow.'

Bob Wood had been leaning over the back of the seat, taking an interest. 'Who comes together?' he asked.

'It's not who,' said Chuck. 'It's *what* comes together.' He saw Bob Wood's puzzled face, and for a moment he wanted to stay silent and keep him out. He was not cruel enough to do it completely. 'We were thinking about the sun and the moon,' he said. 'Coming together. But it's impossible.'

'Well . . .' Bob Wood was thinking, taking it seriously. 'Just about now is the right time for it, I reckon. Full moon tonight, and today's the longest day. Summer solstice. How about that?'

Tessa slapped the diary closed between her hands and stood up. 'I think you're marvellous, Mr Wood! Ain't he marvellous?' She had meant the words for Chuck, but as she spoke she caught his mother's eye and could not look away. Nor could Trudy Hoskins. They gazed at each other, and Tessa, breathlessly, made herself say, 'He is a very nice man, I think.'

And something happened. Trudy Hoskins lowered her eyes and blushed.

24

Fractured Moonlight

Chuck came through the trees so stealthily that Tessa had to put a hand out to touch him and make sure he was not some strange night-walker.

'How did you get out?' she whispered. 'Are they both still there?'

'Talking away like mad downstairs. I put some pillows under my sheet just in case, and then I came out through the front door. They didn't hear a thing.'

'It was worse for me. Jago stayed awake ages.'

They were high on the hill above both houses in a little clearing that let them see the whole valley. It was late, but the sun lingered just below the horizon and the sky was still red when the white disc of the moon freed itself from a distant hillside and lifted against the stars.

With eyes like elves they watched it from their dim glade. 'It's pink,' he said softly. It swam in the outer fringes of the sunset. 'Before long it's going to be right over the place where the sun went down. You were right, Tessa. Gold and silver.'

She was silent for a while, and then she said, 'I wish we could have told them.'

'Bob Wood guessed something was happening. You took his diary and told him the rhyme.'

'I'd have told them everything if it wasn't for you.'

'Well you know what happened when we tried to tell Trudy about going little. She just thought we were making each other worse. Anyway, she's got a lot to talk about— her and Bob Wood.'

'That's what I mean, Chuck. They might believe it now,

135

both of them together.'

'Especially the bit about the man who thinks he can fly,' he said sarcastically. 'And then they'd never give us a chance to get out here. They'd reckon it was too dangerous, or something.'

She sighed. 'Oh, I suppose you're right.'

The valley was a dim and silent cleft. He thought he saw the moon gleam briefly on the stream far below, and he said, 'Don't forget, Tessa, all we're going to do tonight is keep watch. Not going small.'

She nodded, and for the first time shuddered at the thought of what they were doing. They were keeping watch on a man who believed he would be able to fly. Such a man must be dangerous. He was mad.

'But if he does fly,' she said aloud, 'he'll be able to terrify the whole valley.'

'I don't care if he does.' Chuck was looking at the ground at his feet. 'I'm not going to be here much longer anyway.' Already he could feel it slipping away. The little man would prance and pretend, but all the magic would vanish once the house was sold.

'Chuck.' Her voice was very quiet and he turned towards her. 'I don't care about him and flying, but the rest of it is true. We *can* go small, can't we?'

Even in the full glare of the moonlight he could not make out the expression on her pale face. But she was pleading with him to believe what she believed, and suddenly he wanted to be cruel. 'Who knows?' he said. 'Anyway it doesn't matter.' He got to his feet. 'I don't know what you're going to do, but I might as well go home. Nothing's going to happen.' Without bothering to be quiet he plunged down the slope.

He allowed her to catch up with him when he reached the lane in its tunnel of trees.

'Chuck,' she said, 'are you all right?' The fractured moonlight lay about them like white leaves. 'Something's gone wrong, Chuck. What is it?'

'I don't know.'

'Is it me? Have I done anything?'

'No!'

They had been talking softly, but his exclamation was loud and made them both look swiftly down the lane where the man must climb. Nothing stirred. It was still too early. Chuck kept his voice quieter.

'It's not you, Tessa. It's just everything. I don't believe it any more. We're just being crazy. We didn't go little, we only imagined it. Nobody believes it, not even you.'

Bleakness crept into her. The whole of the summer was fading, and going with it was all the magic that lay so thickly in the air it could have lifted her and Chuck across the valley because they had the secret and could use it; all of that was sinking down the dark hillside, draining down and away to be lost for ever.

He kicked the dust and they went through the gate at the side of the house, not caring if they were discovered. It no longer mattered.

They crossed the terrace and stepped down on to the lawn before either of them raised their heads. Tessa understood it first.

'Look,' she said.

The valley had filled. A mist had come with the night, drifting like deep water, submerging rooftops, putting the village out of sight, anchoring itself in treetops and turning the hillsides into islands in a white sea.

'It's still there!' she whispered. 'We haven't lost it.'

The moon was huge, and he saw the thin streaks of high cloud across its face making other islands in the sky. But it was all appearance. If he stepped on to the floor of white that lay across the valley he would plunge through it into streets of houses where people lay asleep. Only his imagination could make it anything else. He began to say so, but she would not let him speak.

'I don't care what happens,' she said. 'I don't care.'

A door opened in the house behind them and a gleam of

yellowish light fell across the lawn, forcing them to step backwards. The door closed, but there was no time to seek the shelter of the apple tree because two people were standing on the terrace with the lawn in full view. The only chance of remaining unseen was to stand still. Chuck saw his mother's dress catch the light and shimmer slightly against the darker figure of Bob Wood. They were talking, but their voices were so low that the words dwindled and, after a moment, ceased altogether.

Tessa never knew what made her turn her back on the terrace. It was certainly no sound for the night was utterly silent, and the figure that stood on the lawn was so still it did not even disturb the wisps of mist that lay around its feet.

25

Bird of Prey

Peregrine Falconer had his back to them. Only his stillness had made him invisible. But now they could see his white hair spread like a bird's mantle on the shoulders of his feathered cloak as he gazed away from them down the valley towards the moon.

The sounds of voices and of footsteps must have reached him but he made no attempt to turn. His arrogant stillness made Tessa shudder and her hand reached to Chuck. He felt the cold touch of her fingers, and his own fear turned around and showed its other face. It became anger. He twisted his head to gaze over his shoulder to where his mother and Bob Wood were standing. It was still her house. Surely she would step forward, call out, do anything to interrupt Peregrine Falconer's performance and destroy whatever ridiculous ceremony was taking place. But neither stirred. They had seen nothing.

Tessa's fingers tightened and pulled him around. The still figure had begun to move. Its head sank, its shoulders came up, and it turned to face them. A change had taken place. It was no longer the head of a man. The curved bill of a huge bird showed against the stars, and the shadows of a hawk's fierce eyes frowned in the faint light. Peregrine Falconer, without them seeing, had put on the hawk helmet. He stepped forward, clothed in feathers. They saw the sheen of them down his sides and heard the scrape of them on the grass, but he did not raise his arms in imitation of a bird in a hopeless attempt to fly. It was worse. He advanced with the rocking walk of a bird and, higher than the crown of his head, his shoulders swayed at every step like hunched wings.

He came to the edge of the pond and paused. Chuck, from the corner of his eye, was aware that the two people on the terrace had at last seen what was happening. His mother shrank back while Bob Wood gave himself space for action just as the hawk's head dipped and the man within its feathers stooped to the water. The bird had lowered its head to drink.

It was then, in the false pause, that Chuck turned completely to face Bob Wood. He had to warn him. The bird would never fly, but within the hooked helmet there was a desperate mad brain.

Only Tessa and Trudy Hoskins saw what happened next. The bird dipped to sip, and the chain around its neck swung forward and touched the water. Small ripples spread outwards, but they were not the only movement. The false eyes, sightless and fixed in the mock bird's head, blinked.

Chuck knew nothing. He did not see the feathered cloak extend itself on the grass, grow sinews and stiffen. All his attention was on Bob Wood. He saw him leave Trudy's side and push forward into dangers he knew nothing about. Chuck had to stop him. He took a step into the open but he was too late. A gust of wind pushed at his back and with it came a sound like a tent clattering in a gale.

He spun round. The moon had gone. The sky was dark as though a tree suddenly stood on the lawn, spreading its leaf-laden branches against the sky. It was a bird. Its vast wings fingered the stars, and as they beat down they raised its body so that its talons danced on the grass.

'No!'

Bob Wood's shout was directed at Chuck. He saw the boy turn to the girl, and then both of them moved forward into the shadow of the wings.

'No!'

They heard him but they paid no heed. As yet the bird was clumsy. There was still a chance.

'The chain!' Tessa's voice was sucked away as the wings swept upwards. 'We've got to get it!'

They put their arms up against the thrust of the wind as the wings beat down. Chuck saw the water roughen.

'Don't look at the pond!'

His yell jerked her head away and she missed the flash of the moon on water. The thrust of the wind made them crouch and, with heads bowed, they faced each other.

'Ready?' she said.

He nodded, and they stood together.

Only the width of the pond separated them from the bird. Its bill was a hook of black iron and its wings were spread to make a canopy under which its prey would die.

'Now!'

Their feet struck the water together, but neither looked down at the splashing silver. They lunged for the chain and saw the second danger when it was too late. The moonlight glinted in the caverns of the hawk's eyes and its glare was sufficient. It had taken on the power to quell and shrank them as they leapt.

Tessa reached for the gold and silver links but failed to touch. She was falling. She saw feathers and the long shank of its leg before a hard surface rushed up out of the darkness and winded her. She slid, unable to prevent herself, down a scaly slope until the ground met her with a second shock. She was slow getting to her feet, and slower still getting her thoughts together. She leant against something as hard and smooth as a boulder, and some distance away another smooth shape curved down into the water's edge.

'Chuck!'

She called with all the power of her lungs but knew her voice was tiny. He was hidden somewhere, diminished to her own size, and perhaps he was injured.

She called his name again but her voice was drowned in a scream that shivered the stars. The falcon was shrieking its triumph over the valley. And the boulder against which she stood tilted. It lifted and she saw what it was. It was a talon of the hawk's foot and it was tearing free of the earth as the wings high above, like the entire sky folding, scooped at the night air. It was about to beat its way into the sky and escape.

She spread her arms against the surface of the talon but it was too smooth and she was too small. It slid from her and there was no grip. She stumbled, knowing she had failed, and when her whole body was jerked sideways she knew that she had been flung aside by the gust of its wings.

But something was hauling her through the air, pressing against her chest so that she could not breathe as she skimmed the tops of the dark grass. The falcon screamed again and the grass fell away, and she was high above ground, held only by the talon's tip where it had hooked into the sleeve of her dress and torn through the material to come out at her neck. She put her arms around the hook and clung.

Chuck's leap took him all the way. His fingers were clutching at the glittering links when the glare of the eyes caught him. Then he was plunging down a steep mountainside, sliding on grey slopes of springy vegetation out towards a sheer drop. He rolled and clutched. Sharp edges bit his hand, but his slide slowed and stopped. He could see nothing. He was within a motionless cascade of grey.

Once he thought he heard his own name called, but it was muffled and distant, and before he could shout a reply, a great scream set the grey cascade shivering and he saw he was in a forest of downward sloping quills and knew where he was. He was trapped in the feathers of the falcon's breast.

26

The Feather

The falcon was the size of a man and clearly visible to the two people standing on the lawn, but to each of them it was something else. Bob Wood saw some primitive type of hang glider lurch upward, and Trudy Hoskins saw a tree thrashing in a sudden gust of wind.

Tessa and Chuck were invisible. He was hidden like a flea in the breast feathers, and she clung to the tip of a talon. Her feet trailed and her legs rapped the ground before she was swung over the edge of the lawn and out into space.

She saw the wings reach once into the sky before the claws closed and put her in a cage made by the talons. It was a cage without safety for there was more than enough space for her to fall between the bars, and the wind of the flight pushed at her, trying to force her out. She eased her torn dress from the black point of the hook, but now there was nothing to hold her except her own grip, and if the talons should open she would slip clear and be lost. She clung, with the wind in her face, and looked down. Far below, a sea of pearly-grey mist lay over the houses and only the spire of the church showed where the sunken village slept.

Chuck was engulfed in the pallid moonlight that filtered through the plumage of the falcon's breast. The feathers pulsed in time to the wingbeats, causing the light to wax and wane, but he was able to see enough to clamber among the quills like a man in the structure of an airship, knowing only that he had to make his way upwards against the direction of the layers. The quills were slippery but the vanes that sprang from them were ridged and gave him toeholds and something to grip, and he worked his way through until the pulsing rise and fall grew greater and he guessed he was directly above the thrusting shoulder muscles. Somewhere nearby lay the chain.

The falcon came up into the face of a breeze and hovered high over its kingdom. Within its talons Tessa saw its tail splay out into a fan of huge oars which pressed down and forward to hold the airstream. The stiff tail feathers touched her claw cage and she reached to where the web of one was split near its quill. She felt it thrum against the air and had both hands wedged in the crevice when the breeze shifted and she was wrenched outwards, swinging helplessly in thin air. It was as though the sail of a windmill had plucked her into the sky.

Her cage vanished as the falcon swung and she was lifted and tossed among clashing vanes as the tail feathers came together and overlapped. She was trapped between them as the falcon narrowed its tail in level flight, and with torn fingers she climbed and clung to its back.

From behind the falcon's head Chuck looked back. Its body stretched away from him like the deck of a boat. But it was a deck without a guard rail and was swept by a tearing gale. Yet something clung there, pressed almost out of sight by the rushing air but inching its way forward. Tessa. A moment later the falcon swung down across the face of the moon, the broad back tilted its shadow and he lost sight of her. When it levelled and moonlight once again racked the length of the deck she was gone.

'Tessa!'

His cry was no sound against the battering of the air but the falcon's head came round. The hard horn of its bill rose like a ship's prow with two enormous painted eyes staring down at him.

Tessa saw it. The sudden tilt of the deck had sent her sliding until, scraping and slipping, she had wedged herself between two smooth plumes. She saw the huge head turn

144

and the black scythe of its bill stab down. Chuck was there. She screamed to warn him, but a new lurch submerged her.

The feathers heaved and threw Chuck sideways. The hook plunged and tore through a foam of quills, ripping into the falcon's mantle as it dug for him. It ploughed once and shaved his leg. He thrust deep into the flimsy cover until he could force himself no further. Not far enough. The next strike would pluck him out. The head lifted, twisted and began its descent. Chuck clutched uselessly at the fronds, wincing to meet the blow. It never came. The falcon, too intent on twisting after its prey, had lost its balance against the breeze and plunged.

Far below, the two figures on the lawn saw the bird stagger in the sky, tilt and fall away. It was no more than a hunting owl.

Tessa was flung forward, slithering down the slope until she lodged among the broken feathers at the falcon's nape. Chuck clutched at her as the stars cascaded by. They were waist deep in a froth of down.

He pointed into the rush of the wind. 'It's there!' he cried. 'I've seen the chain!'

They were flung flat. The wings, half furled, steadied the fall, hung for a moment, and they readied themselves for a new attack. But the falcon, holding the whole valley in its eye, had a more worthy prey than the tiny figures on its back. It closed its wings and dropped.

Black hillsides rocked and swung upwards, then trees and rooftops. Tessa's home. Chuck's house. The falcon checked and screamed. Its head turned and its fierce eyes gazed on them, but it made no attempt to pluck them off. It wanted them there to see its terrible power unleashed.

Its scream, caught in the valley, was flung back at them and the falcon fell.

Crouching and clinging, Chuck saw his mother and the man alongside her. They were motionless as the spread talons swept down on them. Then the wings blotted them out. A jolt as the claws struck, and the muscles of its shoulders churned and it rowed itself into the peak of the sky ready to drop again.

They clung as they were bucked and tossed in the climb and then, in the momentary stillness at the top of its flight, they forced themselves nearer the head. The chain lay there, across the falcon's neck. They saw the square links and the golden hook that passed through one of them. The power lay there, the secret of the falcon's flight. They had to unlock it. There was no other hope.

Chuck stooped to the link. It was as large as himself. He heaved with all his force but the most he could do was lift one end. Tessa, putting her weight against the golden hook, thrust it in Chuck's direction. It was not enough. The hook held.

'Again!'

Chuck's yell once more brought the hawk's head round. In the gape of its bill they saw its pointed tongue curved up as it screamed.

'Now!' Tessa's cry defied it. She had felt the links slide with the bird's movement. And now it was aware of its danger. It speared down at them but they ignored it. The iron point clashed on the chain and their foothold went, but the link lifted. They saw it free itself from its hook as they sprawled in a storm of feathers, knocked backwards by the chain as it parted and the two ends whipped away.

They did not see it fall, nor the falcon's desperate snatch at the links with claw and bill. All they knew was that it shut its wings and dived. They clung to the same quill as the hurricane of the drop lashed it, bending it like a mast in a storm. They could not see. They were thrashed into banks of feathers, then lifted and tossed until their fingers were numb and slipping.

The end was sudden. The feather, loosened by its own lashing, took one last buffet from the gale and broke free.

They fell with it, curving and spiralling, diving before coming up into the breeze with the feather like a shallow boat, hanging on an even keel. It rocked as they helped

146

each other to climb into the broad fan of its ribs and knelt there, drifting down through the night.

On the lawn below, Bob Wood saw the falcon stagger and fall out of the sky. 'That's no bird,' he said. 'Too big and clumsy.'

'It just about blew me off my feet.' Trudy Hoskins was still clinging to his arm. 'It was a whirlwind.'

'Must have been,' he said. 'Lifted the roof off somebody's shed and flung it at us.' There was a gash at their feet where the talons had ploughed through the earth. 'It must have spun off down the valley.'

Bob was laughing at their strange escape in the night when Trudy gave a cry of alarm and ran forward. Two bodies lay motionless on the grass.

High against the stars, Tessa and Chuck had discovered they could steer their boat in the sea of the sky. They shifted their weight and brought its prow up into a faint current of air and rode upwards to float across the face of the moon.

Far away, down through the night they saw the glint of the pond on the lawn and two figures moving. The falcon had failed.

Chuck saw Tessa's hair caught in the breath of air that came over the boat's edge. It was finer than gossamer and paler than a drifting seed.

She felt his eyes on her and she let her long white hair float against the stars. 'We shall soon be down,' she said. 'And then it will be over.'

She put a hand over the edge and let it hang as though she was trailing her fingers in water. 'Maybe,' she said.

They swung their boat and surfed in silence over the glittering mist until they rocked over the lawn and settled.

Somebody was weeping. They saw Trudy crouched over the two still figures that lay on the grass, but they lost sight of her as they tunnelled through the stems.

Tessa was the first to find her own limp hand and climb into it. She dreamt herself awake and found herself lying beside Trudy who was sobbing as she rubbed Chuck's arm and then turned to Tessa as she tried desperately to rouse them.

'It's all right, Mrs Hoskins.' She heard Trudy's gasp as she sat up. 'He'll wake up in a minute.' She held his mother's hand to prevent her moving and to give Chuck time to find himself.

They clung together and after a long moment Chuck stirred and sat up. 'I'm soaked to the skin,' he said.

'I'm not surprised,' said Tessa. 'You fell flat in the pond.'

And then Trudy was hugging both of them so close they had not the breath to say anything.

27

Links

Peregrine Falconer was dead.

People asleep in a cottage at the bottom of the valley heard a tree splinter in the night, but in the silence that followed they had drifted into sleep again. He was not found until next morning, hanging high above ground like a broken bird on a gamekeeper's gallows with the tattered wings of his cloak drooping from the branches.

'They thought he really was a bird at first,' said Tessa. 'A huge grey bird. Until they saw his white hair.'

Coldness clung to Chuck in the heat of the sun. 'I suppose we killed him,' he said.

'I know.'

The coldness reached her, and they fell silent as they stepped from tuft to tuft in the lonely marshland below the village. The sun put pockets of diamonds among the reeds and from time to time she was sure they had found the gold and silver chain for which they were searching, but no dazzle drew Chuck aside. He pressed on as though he already knew where it lay.

'He almost killed your mother and Bob Wood,' she said.

'And he wanted to kill us,' said Chuck.

But that was in the night and far away. Peregrine Falconer was dead in daytime.

'I quite liked him really.' Chuck widened his stride to cross a rivulet where the stream broke up, spreading into the marshes. 'He knew a lot.'

'And now nobody knows anything,' said Tessa. 'Except us.'

Chuck stopped suddenly and stooped to a patch of water

among the reeds. When he stood up he had the chain in his hand with its gold and silver links.

'How did you know where to look?' she asked.

'I know a lot of things.'

He was smiling, and she wrinkled her nose at him. 'Not as much as me. Who told you what had happened to Mr Falconer?'

'You only knew because your granny told you.'

'Everyone thinks he was mad,' she said. 'Trying to fly off the slope with imitation wings.'

Chuck laid the wet chain on a mound of soft grass. It glinted in the sun as though it was hot from the furnace, still molten.

'If he was mad,' he said, 'so are we.'

She picked up the chain. 'Which is why we're not going to tell anybody. Not even about this.'

'Not ever?'

'Not for a long time.'

'But where shall we keep it?'

'You might be clever at finding things, Chuck Hoskins, but sometimes you are very stupid. There's one particular place where this belongs. Come with me.'

They went back upstream and he thought she was taking him to Creance Hall where there was no longer a master for the Falconer mews, but she turned him in the opposite direction and led him up the slope and into the lane where he lived.

'You mean we're going to keep it?' he asked.

She shook her head.

'Are we going to try it in the pond and see what happens?'

'There is no pond.'

He had forgotten that the gash in the lawn had scored right across the dip in the lawn, and the little pond had drained. The Quelling Eye no longer shone.

'What then?'

She paused at his gate, and when she was sure the garden

was deserted she went to the door of his house and tried it. It swung open, and she listened. There was nobody within earshot. 'Where's that photograph your father took?' she said. 'And the map he made?'

He took her across the hall and into the room where the bureau stood in the corner. He gave her the envelope with the map and the picture, and she dropped the chain in beside them and sealed it. 'Now put them in the little drawer,' she said, 'and lock it.'

He did so.

'Now your dad knows,' she said. 'We don't need to tell anybody else. Not yet.'

They came quietly out of the room and stood in the hall under the place where he had fought and killed the spider.

'Is that all, Tessa? Is it over?'

'That sort of thing doesn't end, Chuck. It'll happen again. Next year, maybe.'

'Yes.' There was no Peregrine Falconer to buy the house, so he and Trudy would not be moving away. 'But there's just one thing about last night I can't understand, Tessa.'

'Just one?'

'You needn't smile like that as if you know everything.' But he had to ask the question because only she could answer it. 'Why did Trudy kiss you last night? What did you say to her?'

Suddenly Tessa seemed alarmed. Her eyes were fixed on something behind him, and he twisted around to see what it was. His mother and Bob Wood had come across the lawn and were at the door. They must have heard what he said.

Trudy Hoskins spoke to Tessa. 'Well,' she said, 'aren't you going to tell him?'

Tessa shook her head.

'So it's up to me.' She turned to Chuck. 'I'll tell you. She gave me a feather, that's what she did.'

'That's not much,' he said.

'Oh yes it is. Especially when she said she hoped I was

151

going to be happy; that both of us were going to be happy.'
Trudy was smiling but she was nervous, and she was
blushing.

Chuck bit his lip, and then he said, 'She meant you and
Mr Wood, I expect.'

His mother was holding her breath. 'Yes,' she said.
'About me and Bob. I hope . . .' And then she said no
more, but he knew what was in her mind.

Chuck looked at the man who stood slightly behind her,
a little apart. He was also nervous, but he refused to smile.
Chuck either liked him, or not. He was not going to plead.
His brown eyes, wrinkled deeply at the corners just where
his hair turned grey, waited for Chuck's verdict.

'He ain't bad,' said Chuck.

'You ain't bad yourself,' said Bob Wood.